"Any suggestions where we should look first?" Jason asked Cara.

"The computer," she said. "Anything Dane is working on is there." She pressed her lips together, as if she was tempted to say more.

"Anything else we should know?" he asked.

She shook her head, avoiding his gaze now. Disappointment clawed at him. She was being evasive, either lying or holding something back.

Some people had an instinctive distrust of the law. Other people feared anyone with a badge or shied away out of guilt.

Solving this case would be much easier if he could get Cara to trust him. But he sensed she wasn't one to let down her guard easily. She was going to make him work for any bit of trust he might get.

INVESTIGATION IN BLACK CANYON

CINDI MYERS

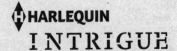

For Carol Berg

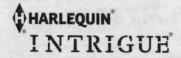

ISBN-13: 978-1-335-13684-8

Investigation in Black Canyon

Copyright © 2020 by Cynthia Myers

Recycling programs
for this product may
not exist in your area.

This edition published by arrangement with Harlequin Books S.A.

For questions and comments about the quality of this book,
please contact us at CustomerService@Harlequin.com.

Harlequin Enterprises ULC
22 Adelaide St. West, 40th Floor
Toronto, Ontario M5H 4E3, Canada
www.Harlequin.com

Printed in U.S.A.

Cindi Myers is the author of more than fifty novels. When she's not crafting new romance plots, she enjoys skiing, gardening, cooking, crafting and daydreaming. A lover of small-town life, she lives with her husband and two spoiled dogs in the Colorado mountains.

Books by Cindi Myers

Harlequin Intrigue

The Ranger Brigade: Rocky Mountain Manhunt

Investigation in Black Canyon

Eagle Mountain Murder Mystery: Winter Storm Wedding

Ice Cold Killer
Snowbound Suspicion
Cold Conspiracy
Snowblind Justice

Eagle Mountain Murder Mystery

Saved by the Sheriff
Avalanche of Trouble
Deputy Defender
Danger on Dakota Ridge

The Ranger Brigade: Family Secrets

Murder in Black Canyon
Undercover Husband
Manhunt on Mystic Mesa
Soldier's Promise
Missing in Blue Mesa
Stranded with the Suspect

The Men of Search Team Seven

Colorado Crime Scene
Lawman on the Hunt
Christmas Kidnapping
PhD Protector

Visit the Author Profile page at Harlequin.com.

CAST OF CHARACTERS

Cara Mead—Dane's administrative assistant at TDC doesn't trust law enforcement, but she's worried enough about her boss to turn to the Ranger Brigade for help.

Jason Beck—The Ranger Brigade's newest member admires Cara's devotion to her boss but is worried Dane Trask may not be as innocent as she claims.

Dane Trask—This former Army Ranger has disappeared in the wilds of Black Canyon of the Gunnison National Park. Why did he leave his job as a successful engineer for TDC Enterprises and abandon those who care about him?

Mitch Ruffino—The TDC vice president alternately praises and condemns Dane Trask, and believes Cara knows more about the situation than she's revealing.

Anthony Durrell and Walter George—Ruffino's muscle take a close interest in Cara. Are they really just two TDC employees or something more?

Chapter One

Sun glinted off the hood of the late-model black pickup, the glare almost blinding. Rocks and cactus ground under the tires as it rolled toward the canyon rim. The walls of the canyon glowed red with the early morning light, in shades from pink and orange and deepest vermillion. But the man behind the wheel had no appreciation for the view. His hands gripping the steering wheel until his knuckles ached, his jaw clenched in concentration, he forced himself to keep his foot on the gas pedal when everything in him screamed for him to put his foot on the brake.

The front tires skidded in loose shale at the canyon's edge and then, in the kind of slow motion he had thought only happened in movies, the truck launched forward, rear wheels momentarily hanging up before the pickup plunged downward. Somersaulting in the clear, thin air before striking the rocks with an impact that sent steel and glass exploding outward, the screech of metal and the shattering of glass reverberated against the granite cliffs.

But there was no one around to hear the crash. No

one to see the truck as it careened off the rock and hurtled into the dark abyss.

CARA MEAD PULLED her Toyota Prius into the visitor's lot near the entrance to Black Canyon of Gunnison National Park. She wiped her sweaty hands on her black slacks and breathed deeply, trying to slow her racing heart. She didn't want to be here, speaking with these people, but she owed it to Dane to try. Something was very wrong and she was determined to keep talking until she found someone who would listen.

Feeling bolstered by the thought, she shoved open the driver's door and stepped out. The intense heat of the Colorado sun was mildly tempered by a stiff breeze that swirled dust across the gravel parking lot and set the small sign at its entrance swinging. Ranger Brigade Headquarters, the sign read. Cara frowned. Was she in the right place? Should she drive to the park headquarters instead and ask to speak to a ranger?

No. She had read enough articles in the local paper to know that the Ranger Brigade was the law enforcement agency charged with investigating crimes on public land in this corner of Colorado. Land that included Black Canyon National Park.

She crossed the lot quickly and pushed open the entrance door to the plain, low-slung building.

A middle-aged woman behind a metal desk looked up. "May I help you?"

"I need to speak to an officer," Cara said. "I need to report a crime."

The woman's eyes behind her blue-framed glasses widened. "I'll see who's available."

She disappeared behind a door and emerged a few moments later with a man in a khaki uniform. Tall and clean-shaved, with short-cropped brown hair, he looked like a law enforcement recruitment poster boy. Though *boy* wasn't exactly the word she would have used, if they had met under different circumstances. "I'm Officer Beck," he said. "How can I help you?"

"I need to report a missing person," she said.

"You might be better off talking to local law enforcement," Officer Beck said. "Would you like me to put you in touch with the sheriff's office?"

"I've already spoken to them," she said. The woman who had taken her report there had showed no sense of urgency. "The person who's missing said he was headed to Black Canyon of the Gunnison. If something has happened to him here, isn't that your concern?"

"Why don't you come back here where we can talk?" He motioned for her to follow him and led her down a short hallway to an unadorned gray-painted room furnished with a table and three chairs. He sat on one side of the table and indicated a chair for her to sit across from him. He waited until she was seated before he spoke again. His eyes met hers. "I'm going to record this for our records. Start with your full name, then tell me who's missing and why you think something might have happened to him."

She had thought Officer Beck was ordinary until that moment—just another jaded man with a badge who had already made up his mind about her and her situation ten seconds after she'd walked into the building. But when Beck's eyes met hers, she felt the jolt of his concern and an almost physical connection that startled her. She glanced at the microphone between them, swallowed hard, then began with, "My name is Caroline Mead—Cara. The person I'm concerned about is Dane Trask. He's my boss at TDC Enterprises. He's been gone two days—and that's really not like him. He hasn't contacted me or anyone else at work. I haven't been able to reach him. None of his neighbors has heard from him. His daughter is out of the country and I haven't been able to reach her, either."

"Maybe he went camping or decided to take a few days to himself."

"But it's not like him to just take off without telling anyone anything."

"Why do you think he's in the national park?"

"The last time I saw him, on Wednesday, about six o'clock, he had his backpack and said he was coming here to the park to hike and try to clear his head. When he didn't show up for work the next day, I knew something was wrong."

Officer Beck plucked a clipboard from the end of the table and took a pen from his shirt pocket. "Let's start with some vital statistics."

Cara gave him the details she had memorized—Dane was forty-one, six feet two inches tall, and weighed one hundred and eighty pounds. He had brown hair and blue eyes, a tattoo of a coiled snake on his right biceps, and he drove a late-model black Ford pickup. That last time she had seen him he'd been wearing sunglasses, khaki hiking pants, hiking boots, a black cotton shirt over a black T-shirt, and was carrying a black backpack.

"Has Mr. Trask ever done anything like this before?" Beck asked. "Gone off and not told anyone?"

"Never. He's always meticulous about giving me his schedule. He's really dedicated to his work and to his volunteer activities. I don't think he's even taken a vacation in the three years I've known him."

Beck nodded. "Was hiking in the park something he did often?"

"Sometimes."

"What kind of shape was he in?" Beck asked. "Do you think he might have been injured or suffered a heart attack or something while he was hiking?"

"He was in great shape." She leaned across the table, searching for the right words to convey just how capable Dane was. "He's a former Army Ranger and he still works out like he could be called back to active duty at a moment's notice. He hikes and runs and bikes and lifts weights. He definitely doesn't look like a desk jockey."

"TDC—that's in that big new building on the edge of the park?" Beck asked.

"Right. They've had a satellite office in Montrose for years, but two years ago they decided to relocate their main headquarters here and built the new campus."

"What kind of work does Trask do there?"

"He's an environmental engineer. TDC does all kinds of infrastructure projects, from building schools and factories to hazardous materials mitigation. There are about three hundred employees at this location, but thousands worldwide."

"And you're his assistant?"

"Administrative assistant." She knew Drew Compton, one of the partners at TDC, still referred to all the admins as secretaries, but his suits still looked like they were out of the eighties, too. She stared into Beck's eyes, determined not to let the intensity of his gaze unnerve her. At least she had the impression he was really listening to her, unlike the woman who had taken her statement at the sheriff's department. "Will you try to find him?"

He sat back and his gaze shifted away. "Do you know if anything was worrying Mr. Trask? Has he seemed preoccupied? Depressed?"

"Not depressed, but he was preoccupied. Something was on his mind, I just don't know what." Dane had been spending more late nights at the office and had been a little absentminded the past couple of weeks, which definitely wasn't like him.

"If you had to guess, what would you say was bothering him?" Beck asked.

"I don't know." She had lain awake much of last night, reviewing every conversation she and Dane had had, searching for any clue as to what might have happened to him. "I thought maybe it was something at work. He's been putting in a lot of late nights and early mornings."

"Was there a specific project he was working on?"

"Several. He did everything from analyzing concrete samples to reviewing environmental testing reports. At any point in time, he might be involved in dozens of jobs."

"What is your relationship with Mr. Trask?"

"He was my boss. And my friend."

"Were you involved with him romantically?"

"No!" She fought down a flush. "Dane and I are both professionals and we had a professional relationship." Yes, Dane was a good-looking, even charming, man. But she had never felt attracted to him romantically and she was sure he felt the same about her. They respected each other and they cared about each other—as friends. Sometimes friendship was even more important than romantic love.

"Was he involved with someone else then—someone who might know better what was bothering him?"

"He wasn't dating anyone at the moment—at least, not that I know of. He ended a long-term relationship with a woman, Eve Shea, last year, though they were still friends. She told me Dane hasn't been in touch with her. His daughter, Audra, is twenty-two. I've been trying to get hold of her, but her voice mail says she's out of town, and she hasn't returned my calls."

"Maybe Mr. Trask is with his daughter."

"He would have told me if he was going away. He had meetings scheduled for the next day and he wouldn't have simply failed to show for them."

Beck seemed to be considering all this. He studied her, not saying anything, until she began to feel uncomfortable, but Cara forced herself to remain still and wait him out. "You really should file a report with local authorities," he said.

"I did," she said. "A woman took my statement, but she didn't seem very concerned. She told me she would put the report on someone's desk, but not to expect to hear anything soon." She pressed her lips together, afraid to say more. She could have told Officer Beck that she had dealt with similar attitudes from law enforcement before. They wouldn't extend themselves to do anything they didn't see as important. The woman at the sheriff's department had sized up Cara as a lovesick admin pining for her hunky boss, who was probably off romancing another woman. She had hoped for better from the Ranger Brigade. "Are you going to look for him?" she asked again.

"We'll look," Beck said. "But you may not like what we find."

Something in his tone chilled her. "What do you mean?"

"One of the sad statistics about national park visitors is that some of them come here with no intention of ever leaving. We have to deal with a number of suicides every year. If, as you say, Mr. Trask was troubled by something…" He let his voice trail away, though his eyes remained locked to hers, watching for her reaction.

She sagged back against the chair. "Dane would never take his own life," she said, her voice shaking. "And when I said he was worried, I didn't mean he was depressed. He was…preoccupied. Like a man trying to figure out a puzzle or solve a problem. That's Dane—he's a problem solver. Suicide wouldn't be a solution to him."

"Then it's possible he met with an accident. He could have fallen and been injured. Some of the terrain in the park can be treacherous. It's one reason we discourage people from hiking alone."

"He told me once that Army Ranger training was all about learning to survive when the odds were against you. If he was injured, he wouldn't give up. He'd try to get to help. Or, if that wasn't possible, he'd wait for help to come to him." She tried to fight back the image of Dane hurt and alone in the wilderness, waiting for more than two days now for someone to find him.

"We'll do our best to search for him," Beck said. "But we have a dozen officers covering more than a hundred and thirty thousand acres of territory, when you consider the park and the surrounding public lands. Did he say where he intended to hike?"

"No." The word was almost a whisper. One man in that vast territory would be so easy to miss.

"We'll start by searching all the trailheads and parking lots for his vehicle. If we find it, that can help narrow the search. And we might be able to borrow a Park Service plane. We can talk to campers and hikers, see if any of them spotted him or—"

A knock on the door interrupted him. "Come in," he called.

The woman who had greeted Cara when she'd entered the Ranger Brigade headquarters eased into the room. She glanced at Cara then addressed Officer Beck. "We just had a call from Mike Griffen at park headquarters. Hikers off Dragon Point spotted a vehicle wrecked in the canyon. He wants someone to go with him to check it out and, since everyone else is away right now…"

Beck stood and, heart in her throat, Cara also rose. "Tell Mike I'll meet him at the overlook," he said.

"What kind of vehicle?" Cara asked.

Beck and the woman stared at her. "He said it was a late-model Ford pickup," the woman said. "The hikers couldn't get close, but they took pictures, and they said it didn't look like it had been there long."

Cara swayed but held steady. Dane might still be all right, trapped in the truck, but alive. She closed her eyes and said a brief prayer.

When she opened them again, the woman had left and Beck was staring at her. He put a hand lightly on her shoulder. "You need to stay here," he said, his voice gentle.

"A late-model Ford truck," she said. "It could be Dane."

"All the more reason for you to stay here."

"Oh no, I'm coming with you." She slung her purse over her shoulder and clutched her car keys. "Just try and stop me."

Chapter Two

Jason Beck squeezed through a narrow opening in the dense underbrush crowding the steep side of the canyon. He and Black Canyon National Park ranger Mike Griffen had spent the last hour and a half hiking down into the canyon, scaling car-size boulders and skidding down gravel washes to the twin music of rushing water and the descending trill of a canyon wren that followed them down. The temperature was at least fifteen degrees cooler here, where the sun's rays rarely reached, with snow still piled beneath the snarled strands of scrub oak and pinyon in mid-April. The brush grew in tangles they had to fight through.

"I'd like to get hold of one of these guys before he decided to drive over the edge and read him the riot act," Mike grumbled as he pushed the branch of a gnarled pinion out of the way. "If they had any idea how much it costs taxpayers to extricate them and their vehicles out of this canyon, maybe they'd go off themselves somewhere else."

"One of the other park rangers told me y'all had to pull a car out of here last year," Jason said.

"Yeah, and one the year before that." Mike removed his hat and mopped sweat from his brow with his shirtsleeve. "I don't get the attraction. It's not like driving off a cliff is a quick or easy way to end it all." He shuddered then pulled a bottle of water from his pack and drank deeply.

Jason drank from his own water bottle and considered the task ahead. The worst thing about a suicide wasn't really finding the body, but telling the family. Cara Mead wasn't related to Dane Trask, but she was the one who had reported him missing, and she was here, so he'd have to break the news to her first. He had tried to persuade her to go home and wait for his call, pointing out that it could take hours to reach the wrecked vehicle and determine the condition of the driver. She had stubbornly refused, so he'd left her waiting in her car at the overlook. At least she had had sense enough not to want to climb down with them.

"You're pretty new on the job, aren't you?" Mike asked.

"I've been here two weeks." Jason answered the next question before it could be asked. "From Washington, DC." He was the first national parks police officer assigned to a duty other than the National Mall. With the growth of the Ranger Brigade task force within Black Canyon of Gunnison National Park and adjacent public lands, his superiors had deemed it time to have one of their own on the team. He'd been their lucky pick.

He would have liked his first case to be something other than a potential suicide.

"This must be a culture shock," Mike said, sweeping his hand to indicate the wild landscape around them.

"Not really," Jason said. "Before I transferred to parks police, I was a ranger at Glacier and Yellowstone."

"No kidding!" Mike grinned. "We'll have to compare notes sometime. I bet we know some of the same people."

"Probably." Jason stowed his water and adjusted his pack. "Ready to keep going?"

"We'd better. When it gets dark down here, you can't see your hand in front of your face." Mike started out again, picking his way along what must have been an animal track. "Hey, I've been meaning to ask," he called over his shoulder. "Who's the woman?"

"She works for the man who may be the owner of this truck," Jason said. "She reported him missing."

"Then she probably saw this coming," Mike said. "In my experience, family and friends usually know something wasn't right, even if they didn't expect suicide."

"She says he wouldn't have killed himself—that he wasn't depressed." Cara's certainty about this had struck him—that, and her insistence that she and her boss weren't romantically involved.

Mike stopped and looked back at him. "Does she think something else happened? That someone else drove him off the cliff?"

The hair on the back of Jason's neck stood up. "She never mentioned anything like that. Maybe it's an accident."

Mike looked up, toward the canyon rim. "To end up down here, someone would have to turn into the overlook and drive across some pretty rough country for several hundred yards. Not impossible, but not likely, either."

"Let's keep going and see what we find."

As they pressed on, Jason distracted himself from the grueling nature of their hike by thinking about Cara Mead. He wouldn't have minded meeting her under better circumstances. The attractive blonde's combination of tender concern and iron determination intrigued him. He'd offended her with his question about her relationship to Dane, but she hadn't let either anger or fear get the best of her. She didn't think much of local law enforcement, but she'd been willing to put her trust in him.

They rounded a bend in the canyon and Mike pointed ahead to a path of broken limbs and scarred earth. "We're getting close," he said.

A hundred yards farther on, they caught their first glimpse of the truck. It lay on its side in the creek, the cab partially crushed, both headlights and all the windows shattered. As they drew nearer, Jason could make out the license plate. "The plate matches the number registered to Dane Trask's vehicle," he said.

"I don't see anyone in the cab," Mike said.

They scrambled the last few yards to the wreck, Jason searching the creek and the surrounding terrain for any sign of a body. When they reached the pickup, Jason leaned into one broken window to look inside. "There's no one in here," he said. "No blood, either. The seat belt isn't broken."

"Maybe he wasn't wearing it," Mike said, coming

up behind Jason. "He might have been thrown clear the first time the truck hit the ground."

They both stared up the steep slope at the tangle of brush and rock. Jason cupped his hands to his mouth. "Dane Trask!" he shouted.

"Dane Trask!" echoed back in a hollow imitation of Jason's voice. As the echo faded, he strained his ears, hearing nothing but the clear, descending notes of the canyon wren.

"What now?" Mike asked.

Jason checked his cell phone. No signal this deep in the canyon. His radio wouldn't work, either. "We'll hike back up and call Ranger Brigade headquarters," he said. "Time to bring in a search dog."

Mike turned to the wrecked truck. "It's going to be a bear of a job getting this truck out of the canyon. We might have to bring in a helicopter."

Jason clapped him on the shoulder. "I'll leave that to you." He pulled a camera from his pack. "I'd better take some photos, just in case this turns out to be a crime scene."

"If you do find the guy alive, let me know," Mike said. "I'll haul him in for trashing the canyon."

Jason squinted through the viewfinder at the mangled vehicle. If Dane Trask had gone over the edge in this truck, it would be a miracle if he was still alive. And Mike wouldn't be the only one standing in line to ask him questions.

CARA HAD PULLED her car into the meager shade of a pinion at the overlook and sat in the driver's seat, phone in hand, reviewing every text message she'd had from Dane over the past two weeks. Messages about schedule changes, meetings he wanted her to add to his calendar, a lunch order he'd asked her to pick up. Ordinary business-related correspondence.

Yet she couldn't shake the feeling that he had been distracted by something. His mind sometimes wandered when she was talking to him, and too many nights when she left work he was still hunched over his desk, staring at his computer monitor or at stacks of printouts. When she'd ask what he was working on, he would shrug off the question. "Just reviewing some data. Have a good evening."

She checked the time. Almost four hours had passed since she had followed Officer Beck and a park ranger to the overlook. "You should go home," Beck had said. "I promise I'll call as soon as we know something."

At home she would only pace and fret—essentially what she was doing here. But here she could see with her own eyes what was happening, and not have to rely on an officer who might not want to give her all the details. Beck might even think he was protecting her from ugly reality, but she was an adult. She didn't need protecting. She had seen ugly before, and she knew it was better to face it than to pretend.

She shoved open the car door and walked down a short trail to the edge of the overlook. The wild beauty of this place drew visitors from all over the world. They came to marvel at the deep chasm sliced into the high desert landscape, with its painted granite and sandstone cliffs and abundant wildlife. But Cara didn't see the beauty today—she only saw the danger in a canyon so remote and full of hazards. She hugged her arms across her chest and closed her eyes, focusing on the warmth of the sun beating down on her skin, the scent of pine and sage on the breeze that caressed her cheek, and the utter silence and peace of the afternoon. Dane was tough. He had skills and he was at home in wild places. If anyone could survive out here, it would be him.

Feeling calmer, she turned and walked back up the trail to her car. When she opened the driver's-side door a few minutes later, something on the seat made her catch her breath. She scooped up the object—a bright red USB flash drive, about two and a half inches long. Despite the heat of the day, a chill shuddered through her.

"Cara!"

Clutching the drive, she whirled to see Officer Beck striding toward her, his tall frame and broad shoulders silhouetted in the late-afternoon sun. He looked scarcely winded by the hard climb out of the canyon, though, as she moved closer to him, she saw the sheen of sweat at the open collar of his shirt and the torn sleeve of his uniform. "Dane?" The single syllable was all she could manage, fear clogging her throat.

Beck shook his head. "We didn't find him. The license plate on the truck is registered to him, and the description fit, but we didn't find anyone down there—dead or alive."

She swayed, her knees weak, whether with relief he hadn't found a body or fear of Dane still down there somewhere, suffering, she couldn't say. Beck put out a hand to steady her and led her back to her car. He pushed her gently into the driver's seat then pulled a bottle of water from his pack and offered it to her. "You've been waiting a long time," he said. "That's not easy."

She sipped the water, trying to pull herself together. "I was trying to prepare myself for the worst," she said.

"This doesn't mean he's alive," Beck said, his eyes intent on her. "He could have been thrown from the truck on the way down."

She handed the water bottle back to him. "What are you going to do now?"

"We're going to bring in a dog to search for him. And we'll have people looking, too." He looked toward the sun, sitting low on the horizon. "We've got less than an hour of daylight left. We may have to continue the search in the morning."

She nodded, still reeling from the news that Dane's truck was in the bottom of the canyon—without Dane.

"You need to go home now," Beck said. "There's nothing else you can do here. I can get someone to drive you."

"I can drive myself." She swung her feet into the car and reached for the button to start the engine. Only then did she remember the flash drive and let out a surprised "Oh!"

Beck stiffened. "What is it?"

She held out her hand, the flash drive lying on her palm. "I got out of the car just now and walked to the edge of the canyon to look down," she said. "When I came back, this was on the driver's seat."

He frowned at the flash drive. "Could it have fallen out of your purse or your pocket?"

She shook her head. "It's not mine. I'm sure of it."

"Then whose is it?"

She swallowed hard. He wasn't going to believe what she had to say—she didn't believe it. "Look at it again," she said.

His gaze returned to the drive. "There's some kind of logo on it—WHW."

"Welcome Home Warriors. It's the veteran's organization Dane founded. He gave these out all the time to promote the cause."

Beck's eyes met hers—skeptical, but not completely disbelieving. "You think this flash drive belonged to Dane Trask?"

"I think he left it for me," she said. "I think he's still alive. And he was right here."

Chapter Three

The sick feeling that had filled Jason when Cara Mead
had showed him the flash drive stayed with him all
the way back to Ranger headquarters. He'd felt real
sympathy for her up until that moment. All right, if he
was being honest, he'd been pretty taken with her, had
thought he'd even like to know her better. Being new
in town, he didn't know many people outside of the office, and she was pretty and close to his own age. He'd
been thinking he might ask her out.

When she'd come up with that wild story about the
flash drive and her boss having put it in her car, he'd
realized she might be just another nutcase. He'd met
plenty of them in his job, attention seekers or the truly
delusional. He just hadn't expected it from such a pretty
young woman.

He parked his black-and-white SUV in front of the
long, low building near the entrance to Black Canyon
of Gunnison National Park and crossed the gravel lot to
the door. A United States flag snapped in a stiff breeze
on a pole at the corner of the building, and a profusion

of purple lupines rippled in the wind, their candy-sweet smell drifting to him.

After five years patrolling the National Mall, the vast emptiness and stark beauty of the high desert country around the canyon still moved him. Everything was so different here. Maybe that's why he had thought the people would be, too.

He pushed open the door and stepped into an office filled with activity. Officer Carmen Redhorse looked up from the copy machine. "What have you got there?" she asked.

He looked down at the evidence bag that contained the flash drive. Cara Mead hadn't wanted to give it to him, but he'd insisted. It was evidence in this case, though evidence of what, he wasn't sure. "A woman came in to report her boss was missing in the canyon," he said. "She says this belonged to him." No need to go into the whole story now. "While she was here, a report came in from the park that they'd found a vehicle off Dragon Point. Turned out it was the missing man's vehicle, but no sign of him."

Carmen grimaced. "He could be anywhere down there if he was thrown from the car when it went over," she said.

"It was a truck, but yeah. The park rangers are still looking." He glanced at the flash drive. "I doubt this will be much help, but I figured we'd better take a look."

"Let's see what you've got." Officer Mark Hudson approached. Like Jason, he was a newer addition to the force, replacing the former tech expert who, the story went, had married an heiress he'd met while on a case and relocated to Los Angeles to start a charitable organization devoted to helping street kids. "Hud" had come to the Ranger Brigade from the DEA, and had a reputation as a tech wiz.

Jason followed Hud to a desk on the far side of the open office space. Hud settled in a chair in front of a laptop and pulled on a pair of gloves. He then carefully removed the drive from the evidence bag and inserted it in the port on the side of the computer. A few keystrokes later and a series of numbers filled the screen.

Jason leaned over Hud's shoulder and studied the numbers: 25.5, 16, .72. "Any idea what we're looking at?" he asked.

Hud hit a few keys and a spreadsheet with letters and numbers appeared on the screen: 3H, 18.O, 2H, H_2SO_4 and others. The columns to the left were filled with more numbers.

"I think these are chemical notations," Hud said. "Sulfuric acid is H_2SO_4. I think 2H is deuterium. So maybe the numbers are percentages or something. What kind of work did the missing man do?"

"He's an environmental engineer for TDC Enterprises."

Hud tapped a few keys and more letter-and-number combinations replaced the first. "That fits," he said. "This looks like some kind of report. Maybe a chemical analysis."

"But an analysis of what?" Jason asked. And was it just nonsense Cara Mead had thrown together to try to keep his attention on her, or real evidence in this case?

"I'll print this out," Hud said. A few seconds later, the printer adjacent to his desk whirred to life.

"TDC Enterprises has that big campus right on the edge of the park," Lieutenant Michael Dance said as he joined them. One of the original members of the Ranger Brigade, he'd come to the squad from Customs and Border Protection. "Is that why this woman thought he disappeared here?"

"She said the last time she saw him, he was headed into the park," Jason said. "He liked to hike here."

Hud removed the drive from the computer, returned it to the evidence bag then stripped off the gloves. "What was her reaction when you told her his truck was at the bottom of the canyon?" he asked.

"She thinks he's still alive." He nodded toward the evidence bag. "She was waiting up top while a park ranger and I hiked down to check on the truck. When we got back, she said she found that on the front seat of her car. She thinks the missing man—Dane Trask—left it for her. That it's a clue."

"Welcome Home Warriors," Carmen said. She joined the group by Mark's desk.

"That's what it says on the drive—WHW," Jason said.

"Dane Trask was involved with that group," Carmen said. "I met him when he and my husband worked an event together. WHW hosted a bunch of veterans for a week of hiking and rafting and stuff like that." She glanced at Jason. "My husband, Jake, served in Afghanistan. He'll be upset to hear Dane is missing. He'll want to help."

"Jake works for Colorado Parks and Wildlife," Dance explained to Jason and Hud. "He'll be good if we need to conduct a search."

"If the park service doesn't come up with anything, they may ask for our help," Jason said. "In the meantime, I want to talk to Dane Trask's daughter."

"If he has a daughter, why didn't she report him missing?" Hud asked.

"That's one thing I want to find out," Jason said.

"Did this woman—who was she again?—give you any other information that might be useful?" Dance asked.

"Her name is Cara Mead. She's Dane Trask's administrative assistant at TDC," Jason said. "She said he'd been preoccupied with something at work, but he wasn't the type to take his own life."

"And she said he left this flash drive in her car while you were down in the canyon?" Hud asked.

"Yeah. But that's crazy, right?" Jason said. "According to her, he sneaked up there while she was standing out at the overlook, then left without trying to talk to her or anything."

"That overlook is three hundred yards from the parking area," Dance said. "You can't see the road from the overlook because of the way the terrain slopes away. So it's not impossible."

"But why do something like that?" Jason asked.

"Maybe he's hiding from someone, or running from someone," Carmen said.

"It might be worth talking to her again," Hud noted. "Find out what that report on the flash drive means."

"Or come right out and ask her if she made the whole thing up," Dance said.

Jason nodded. They were right. He needed to talk to Cara again. But he wasn't looking forward to finding out she might really have been lying to him.

CARA HAD BEEN calling Audra Trask's cell phone for the past couple of days, getting a Mailbox Full message ever since this morning. Desperate to talk to Dane's daughter, she drove to Audra's building and climbed to the second-story apartment.

Audra Trask, a cloud of messy dark hair framing delicate features, answered the door with what looked like a half-eaten cheeseburger in one hand and a large soft drink in the other. Her eyes widened when she saw Cara. "Oh my gosh—your phone call! I swear I was going to call you back first chance I had, but things have been so crazy around here." She held the door open wider. "Come on in."

Not waiting for a reply, she turned and walked back into the living room, where unopened mail covered the coffee table and the sofa was all but obscured by mounds of clothing. "Sorry the place is such a mess, but I just got home and between jet lag and having been away ten days, I barely know which end is up."

"Where were you?" Cara asked.

Audra stuffed the last bite of cheeseburger in her mouth and chewed before she answered. "Sorry, I was starved. And I've been craving an American fast-food burger for at least the last week."

At Cara's blank look, she added, "I was in Paris and

my cell phone didn't work over there. I know your message said it was urgent, but I figured I couldn't really do anything until I got home anyway, so…" She frowned. "What's wrong? You look upset."

Not wanting to panic Audra, Cara hadn't mentioned Dane, only that she needed to hear from Audra right away. "Have you heard from your father?" she asked.

"Dad? No, why?" Before Cara could answer, Audra's face paled. She clutched Cara's arm. "Is he okay? Was there an accident? Is he in the hospital?"

This was the other reason Cara hadn't been more specific on the phone: Audra was excitable and had a very active imagination. She took Audra's hand and led her to the sofa, pushed aside a pile of clothes and urged her to sit. "Two days ago, your dad left the office and said he was going hiking in Black Canyon of the Gunnison," Cara said. "As far as I can determine, he hasn't been seen or heard from since."

"Oh my gosh! Did he fall or something? I know they say you're not supposed to go hiking by yourself, but Dad did it all the time and he's…well, he's Dad."

As in Dane the former Army Ranger. Dane who could do anything. Cara squeezed Audra's hand, silencing the flow of words. "We don't know what happened." She swallowed hard but forced herself to continue. "His truck was found at the bottom of the canyon this evening. Dane wasn't in it, and there was no sign of him."

For once, Audra didn't have anything to say. She stared, mouth open, eyes wide and troubled.

"I think he's still alive," Cara hastened to add. "And

probably okay. While I was out at the park, away from my car, someone left one of those Welcome Home Warriors' USB flash drives he's always giving out on the front seat of my car. I think it was your dad."

"Why would he leave a flash drive in your car?" Audra asked. "Why not a note?"

"I don't know," Cara said. Maybe Dane was in danger and the flash drive was the only way he could think to communicate. But she didn't mention this to Audra.

The doorbell rang. Audra looked toward the door but made no move. "Are you expecting someone?" Cara asked.

"Not really. But when my friends hear I'm back in town, one of them might stop by." She shoved to her feet and went to peer out the security peephole. She turned back to Cara, eyes wide. "It's two cops."

Cara stood, also. "You'd better let them in."

If Officer Beck was surprised to see Cara with Dane's daughter, he didn't let the emotion show on his face. He merely nodded to her, then stepped aside to let the other man with him move forward. Blond and blue-eyed, this new man, also dressed in the khaki uniform of the Ranger Brigade, introduced himself as Officer Mark Hudson. "Officer Beck and I would like to ask you some questions about your father, Dane Trask," he said to Audra.

Beck turned to Cara. "We won't keep you," he said.

She debated pretending not to take the hint, but she was so drained by the day's events she decided to save the argument for another time. She could call Audra later to find out what the two Rangers wanted.

She'd leave quietly now, but she hoped the handsome cop didn't get the idea she would just as willingly stay away from his investigation.

AUDRA STARED AT Hud for so long that Jason wondered if she remembered there was another person in the room. He cleared his throat and she flinched, as if startled. "Cara told me my dad's truck somehow ended up in the bottom of Black Canyon and nobody has seen or heard from him for two days." She clutched her head with both hands, tousling her wild mane of dark hair even further. The hair was the only thing big about her. She was small-boned and fine-featured, only a little over five feet tall, and slender. "I've been out of the country for the past ten days—in Paris, visiting friends. To come home to this is just so disorienting."

"Why don't we sit down and talk?" Hud touched her arm and led the way to the sofa, which was buried under mounds of clothing.

"Oh gosh, I'm so sorry." Audra began gathering armfuls of clothing and tossing them onto the room's only chair, which was already covered in garments, so that most of the new ones slid in a heap to the floor.

"It's okay," Jason said. "Let's just sit and talk."

"When was the last time you saw or heard from your father?" Hud asked when they were all seated—Hud and Audra next to each other on the sofa, Jason perched on the coffee table.

"The day before I left for Paris. He took me to dinner that night, as kind of a celebration, you know?"

"What took you to Paris?" Hud asked. "Just a vacation, or business?"

"Not business." She laughed. "I run a preschool and childcare center. Friends from college live in Paris and they've been after me to come see them for ages. I had to save for, like, two years to afford the trip, so it was kind of a big deal."

"How did your father seem to you?" Jason asked. "Was he upset or did he seem preoccupied?"

"I don't think so," she said. "But then, I was so excited about the trip that I might not have noticed."

"Did you notice anything unusual?" Hud pressed.

"Not really." She wrinkled her forehead.

"What is it?" Jason leaned toward her.

"It's just…well, right before he left, he told me to be careful." She shrugged. "He always told me to be careful, so I just smiled and said, 'Sure, Dad.' Instead of telling me goodbye and leaving, he grabbed my hand and looked me in the eye and said, 'I mean it. You be careful—in Paris and after you get home.'"

Chapter Four

Intuition wasn't something that played well in court or carried much weight on paper, but Jason had learned to trust his own instincts when it came to investigations. Audra Trask's statement that her father had warned her to be careful seemed innocent enough, but Jason had a sense it could be significant. "What did he want you to be careful of?" he asked.

She shook her head. "I don't know. He's always been very protective of me. When I was a teenager, I loathed it, but now that I'm older, I think it's really sweet. But this was over the top, you know?"

"Do you think he told you that because he was afraid of something?" Jason asked.

She frowned, and didn't say anything for a long time. "That's hard for me to answer," she said after a moment. "He's my dad, and kind of my hero. A little larger than life." Her smile carried the suggestion of apology. "It's immature, I guess, but I always think of my father as someone who isn't afraid."

"Would you say you and your father are close?" Hud asked.

"Yeah." She smiled, and the effect was pretty breath-taking. Jason thought Hud's eyes might have glazed over for a bit. "It's funny, really," Audra said. "I mean, he and my mom never married and, for big chunks of my childhood, he was deployed and I didn't see him. But he's always worked hard to be part of my life." The smile melted away. "What do you think has happened to him?"

"How often do you usually see your father or talk to him?" Hud asked.

"We have lunch or dinner at least once a week when we're both in town," she said. "And we talk or text almost every day. Except not while I was in Paris. My cell phone didn't work there, and I didn't want to bug my friends to use theirs all the time. I knew I'd see him when I got home." Her expression clouded and she bit her lip.

"What's your relationship to Cara Mead?" Jason asked.

The question pulled her back from the brink of a breakdown. "Cara? Well, we're friendly, but we're not really friends. I mean, she works for my dad, so I talk to her when I stop by his office sometimes, but we don't socialize or anything."

"What about she and your dad?" he asked. "Do they socialize?"

"You mean date?" Audra shook her head, hair whipping around. "Maybe he'll take her to lunch on her birthday or something, but they aren't, like, a couple."

Jason relaxed and ignored the way Hud was staring at him.

"What happened to my dad's truck?" she asked. "How did it end up at the bottom of the canyon?"

"We think someone drove or pushed it over," Hud said.

She looked confused. "But who would do something like that? And where was my dad?"

"Your father served in the military, on active duty, I understand," Hud said.

She nodded. "Yes. He was in Iraq and Afghanistan. With the Army Rangers."

"Did he have any trouble readjusting to civilian life after he was discharged?" Hud asked.

"Not that I'm aware of. I mean, he doesn't talk about his service much, but I don't think he ever struggled with PTSD or anything like that."

"Any history of depression?" Hud asked.

"No." She leaned forward and actually grabbed his wrist. He leaned back, startled, but she held on. "You think he committed suicide? Well, he didn't. He isn't like that."

Hud looked at Jason. Audra still had a grip on him that was probably uncomfortable, though probably not dangerous. Jason took the evidence bag with the flash drive and passed it to her. "Have you ever seen this before?" he asked.

She let go of Hud to accept the package. "Dad gives these out to lots of people," she said. "I have one around here somewhere."

"Can you think of anyone else who might know where your dad is or what he's doing?" Hud asked. "Anyone he might have confided in?"

"Not really. I mean, he has lots of friends, but he isn't the type to spill his guts to other people. I mean, most guys aren't, right?"

"What about girlfriends?" Jason asked.

"He hasn't dated anyone since Eve."

"Eve?" Hud asked.

"Eve Shea. His ex-girlfriend. They were together three years before they split up. She wanted to get married and have babies, and he didn't want that. They're still friends, but I don't think he would have confided in her."

They asked a few more questions about Dane's state of mind, where he might have gone, et cetera. But Audra Trask didn't appear to know anything helpful. At last, both officers stood and Audra walked with them to the door. "If you think of anything, call us anytime, night or day," Hud said, handing her his and Jason's business cards.

"I will."

They left her studying the cards. Unlike Cara, she didn't demand to be kept up to date on any information they found. She probably trusted them to tell her what she needed to know.

Back in the parking lot, Hud said, "Anyone could have left that flash drive."

Jason nodded. "But a random stranger leaves a flash drive that once belonged to Dane Trask in the car of his administrative assistant, who has just reported Trask missing—while I'm down in the canyon checking out Trask's wrecked truck?"

"So, yeah," Hud agreed, "not a random stranger. Someone who knew Dane."

"Someone who knows something about his disappearance," Jason said. "Someone who knew who Cara was, and why she was at the park."

"Dane would know that. Who else?"

"That's what we need to find out."

SATURDAY MORNING, Jason stood at the Dragon Point overlook with Lieutenant Randall Knightbridge and his search dog, Lotte. The dog and her handler had returned only that morning from a training exercise outside Denver. Lotte, a fawn-colored Belgian Malinois with black-tipped fur and movie-star eyes, kept her gaze fixed on Knightbridge as he approached, one of Dane's worn gym socks, which Cara had retrieved from a gym bag in his office, in a plastic pouch in his hand. He unsealed the bag and held it open while she shoved her nose inside. "Seek!" he commanded.

The dog took off, nose scanning back and forth across the dry earth around the overlook. Nearby, a few early tourists looked on curiously. The faint track where the truck had driven over the cliff was still visible in a few spots, but an onlooker would have to know what had happened to realize what he or she was looking at. The bare rock around much of the area obscured the true nature of the tragedy.

Lotte circled around them, whining. "She's not picking up anything," Knightbridge said. He looked around the area. "It's been—what?—at least three days since that truck went over. Lots of traffic here, not to mention the bare rock doesn't hold scent well."

"So maybe Dane was here with the truck and maybe he wasn't." Jason rubbed the back of his neck. "And maybe he was here Friday when we found the truck—when his assistant says someone left that flash drive in her car."

"Lotte has an excellent nose, but she's not a miracle worker," Knightbridge said. He whistled to the dog and she trotted back to his side. "Let's head into the canyon. If this guy is anywhere, he's there."

The National Park had decided to stop issuing permits to hike and camp in the inner canyon at least until the truck was pulled out. In addition to the possibility that a curious hiker would compromise a crime scene or even vandalize the truck, park authorities didn't want to deal with the trauma of someone potentially finding Dane's body. Much better to leave that to the professionals.

As a National Parks Ranger, Jason had seen his share of dead bodies, mostly heart attacks and victims of falls, but there had been one suicide. It wasn't something he liked to think about. But it was important to Trask's family, and to the case, to try to find him, whether he was dead or injured, or fleeing a crime or an enemy.

"Believe it or not, I've only been down here one other time in the past three years," Knightbridge said as they navigated the steep trail into the inner canyon. They descended through thick stands of stunted pinyon and juniper trees and prickly Gambel oak, then through a grove of aspen, the leaves stirring like a crowd of whispering children in the hot breeze.

"I was here yesterday when we found the truck," Jason said. His thighs still ached from the steep climb.

"Who needs a gym, right?" Knightbridge asked, though his bulging biceps suggested he lifted weights on a regular basis.

"I said I was looking for work that was a little more physical than patrolling the National Mall," Jason said, skirting around a boulder and pushing past a tree branch.

"Most of the action is up top," Knightbridge said. "And most of it isn't in the national park. The Curecanti National Recreation Area and Gunnison Gorge are more remote, so people tend to think they can get away with crime there. Sometimes they do, but we do our best to stop them."

"I'm still trying to figure out the crime in this case," Jason said. "Is Dane Trask a suicide victim? Or a murder victim? Or did he try to fake his own death? And why? Is he running from a crime he committed, or from something else?"

"Maybe we have to find him to figure any of that out," Knightbridge said. "What does his family say?"

"His daughter's been out of the country and doesn't know much," he said. "I talked to his ex-girlfriend this morning, but they split up months ago and she says, as far as she knew, everything was fine. I haven't found anyone else he's close to, except his administrative assistant, who first reported him missing."

"Maybe Lotte will help us get some answers."

At the sound of her name the dog, who had been bounding ahead of them down the narrow trail, turned and looked toward them, mouth half open in what really wasn't a smile but looked like it. Maybe Jason should get a dog now that he was living in a place with so many trails and parks to explore. His rental was awfully empty with just him rattling around in there.

He'd like to start dating again. He'd been friends with a lot of women in DC, but nothing had ever clicked with any of them. Too bad the one woman who really interested him since he'd moved to Colorado was involved in this case. Not that anything prevented him from asking her out, but she didn't seem to have a very high opinion of law enforcement in general, so why set himself up for failure?

Approximately an hour and a half after starting out, they reached the canyon and hiked another half hour along the river to reach the site of the wreckage. Knightbridge dug the bag with Dane's sock out of his pack and commanded Lotte to "Seek!"

The dog began scanning the ground around the wreckage, tail wagging.

"If she finds him, I hope he's still alive," Knightbridge said. "She gets depressed when she finds someone dead. It's the downside to being a search and rescue dog—she likes the rescue part. So do I, for that matter."

"Have you done much of this kind of work?" Jason asked. He hadn't yet spent much time with the lieutenant, who stood out among the other Rangers with his full-sleeve tattoos. "Looking for missing people in the park?"

Knightbridge nodded. "Too much. Most of the time it's just a kid or hiker who wandered off course and we find them okay. But sometimes there's no happy ending." He glanced at Jason. "Suicides are the worst."

Jason nodded. "I guess people like all this wide-open space, where their family doesn't have to find them."

"But we do." Knightbridge nodded toward the searching dog. "We did a search like this two years ago. A guy from Sweden, of all places, rented a car in Denver, drove all the way out here and went off near Tomichi Point. He mailed a letter to his brother back in Stockholm, telling him what he intended to do. The brother got the letter five days later, called us and we went searching. We found the car quick enough—it was equipped with locater technology. But we had to get Lotte to find the body." He grimaced. "It was an awful mess."

They watched the dog continue to search. "Can she find anything after this much time?" Jason asked.

"We haven't had any rain or much foot traffic down here," Knightbridge said. "And the ground is wetter here near the river, so it holds scent better. So there's a good chance she'll pick up something."

As if to confirm his assessment, Lotte headed for the wrecked truck and began nosing around the door. Knightbridge followed and wrenched the door open for her. The dog stood with her front paws on the truck's footboard, sniffing the interior.

"We know it's Dane's truck," Jason said. "Of course his scent is going to be inside."

"Seek!" Knightbridge commanded again.

The dog retraced her steps, scanning the ground all the way around the truck. Finally, she returned to Knightbridge and sat at his feet, looking at him alertly. "She's not finding anything," he said. "Either Dane Trask was thrown from the truck before it ever got down here, or he wasn't in it when it went over the edge."

Jason looked up toward the rim of the canyon far above. "Start the engine, get the vehicle headed downhill and jump back," he said.

"Waste of a nice truck." Knightbridge fed Lotte a handful of treats from a pouch on his belt.

Jason walked around the vehicle, examining it more closely than he had the day before when he had been focused on looking for a person trapped in or beneath the wreckage. Parts of the vehicle were bashed in by collisions with rocks or trees on the way down, while other sections were relatively unharmed. The truck bed, though twisted to one side, was intact, the tailgate still latched.

Knightbridge peered into the truck bed. "What's that?" he asked.

Jason moved to stand beside the lieutenant and stared at the bright yellow bandana lying crumpled in the bed of the truck. "That wasn't there yesterday," he said. No way he and Griffen would have missed it.

Knightbridge lowered the tailgate and climbed into the bed of the truck. "There's something wrapped up in it," he said. He knelt and carefully teased apart the folds of fabric. "It's another one of those flash drives."

Jason studied the blue drive, the WHW logo in script across the plastic casing.

"That bandana has the logo for TDC all over it," Knightbridge said.

Jason shifted his attention to the yellow bandana and a shiver ran through him. "That's not the only thing on it," he said. "If I'm right, that stain on the back is someone's blood."

Chapter Five

Cara yanked another weed from the raised garden bed in the backyard of the little Victorian bungalow she was trying to transform into her home. Demolishing a wall or ripping out plumbing would have been a more satisfying way to work off her frustrations, but she had finished all of that type of work last month and was into the rebuilding phase, so she had turned her attention to this future vegetable and flower garden. With every dig and pull at a stubborn clump of weeds, she imagined yanking on a certain smug Ranger's head.

She'd actually believed Officer Jason Beck—as Audra had referred to him—might be different from most of the other lawmen she'd dealt with. He'd listened to her concerns about Dane and had seemed to really care.

Then she had showed him that flash drive and his reaction told her he'd thought she was crazy. Or worse, a liar. When she'd talked to Audra earlier that morning, her impression of him hadn't improved. Apparently, he'd spent part of Audra's interview insinuating that there must be something going on between Cara and her boss.

She wrapped her hand around a thick tuft of foxtail and gave it a savage pull, blinking back tears. Jason Beck wasn't worth crying over. She'd wanted to trust him, but he was just like the others—the cops in Houston who had brushed her off when she urged them to do more to track down her brother's murderer. Sure, Corey had been an addict who had been in and out of trouble for years. He'd probably been killed by someone who'd supplied him drugs. But that didn't mean his murderer didn't deserve to be punished.

Those cops hadn't showed much interest in finding justice for Corey. His murderer had never been found and, even after almost three years, the knowledge still hurt.

And it had hurt to see the concern in Jason's eyes turn to wariness as he had looked at the flash drive and listened to her story about it appearing on her car seat, a message from Dane. He had looked at her the way those cops in Houston had—as if she and her concerns didn't matter.

She tugged hard at a clump of dandelions and they came free, dirt flying, rocking her back on her heels. She brushed a clump from her face and winced as it smeared. Just then the thud of a car door closing made her whip her head around. A pair of long, khaki-clad legs headed her way. She shoved to her feet and faced Ranger Jason Beck.

"Ms. Mead." He inclined his head, and she straightened, resisting the urge to scrub at the dirt on her cheek and brush dried grass from her jeans. She didn't need to pretty herself up for him.

She said nothing, the silence stretching awkwardly between them, his brown eyes studying her. Evaluating. Heat spread through her and her skin prickled with awareness, as if his gaze was a physical touch.

"I took a look at that flash drive," he said finally.

"Yes?"

"I'm going to need your help figuring out what it means."

She hadn't expected that—asking for her help. "Sure. Uh, I guess you'd better come inside."

She turned, aware of him following her into the house. She stopped in the entryway to toe off her sneakers then went into the kitchen, where her laptop was already set up and running. She pulled out the chair and pointed to the one adjacent. "You can sit there."

A voice in her head nagged that she should offer him a glass of water or something, but she ignored it. This wasn't a social visit. "Let me see the drive," she said.

He took the drive in its small plastic bag marked "Evidence" from his shirt pocket and laid it beside her computer. "I'm going to have to handle it to insert it into the USB port," she said.

"It's okay to touch it," he said. "We already checked for prints."

She leveled her gaze at him. "And?"

Clearly, he didn't want to tell her, but she held his gaze and didn't move. A hint of red came to his cheeks. "We didn't find any," he said.

Triumph surged through her. He was stubborn, but so

was she, and she wasn't going to let him get away with withholding information that could pertain to Dane's disappearance. She pulled the drive from the bag and clicked it into the port on the side of her laptop. A message flashed on the screen: How do you want to open this file?

She highlighted the first choice, Excel, and a spreadsheet filled the screen. Jason moved his chair until he was seated right beside her, his shoulder brushing her arm as he leaned forward to study the display. "What are we looking at?" he asked. "Do you know?"

"It's a water quality analysis." She pointed to the left-hand column. "These are the elements tested for." She slid her finger to the next column. "These are the quantities found in the sample, expressed as parts per million, compared to acceptable levels in this final column."

"Most of the numbers in that last column are zeroes," he said.

"Right. Because most of this is nasty stuff you don't want to find in water."

He nodded, brow furrowed. "So what is all this nasty stuff?" he asked.

"Thorium, uranium, deuterium—the first two are radioactive to varying degrees. And then there's arsenic, mercury and lead. Those can kill you, or at least make you very sick."

He sat back and continued to stare at the screen. She turned in her chair to study him. He wasn't movie-star gorgeous, but he had strong features she found attractive—Roman nose, square chin, deep-set dark eyes with dark eyebrows and dark lashes that she, as a pale blonde, envied. He shifted his gaze and met hers, and her cheeks heated, embarrassed to be caught staring.

"Where is this report from?" he asked.

She turned her attention to the screen once more. "There's no information about that. The header is missing. I think this is just a section cut and pasted from a larger report."

"And you said this USB was lying on the front seat of your car when you returned from the overlook?"

"I said it because it's true."

His frown deepened. "Your car wasn't locked?"

"No. I only stepped away from it for a few minutes and there was no one around."

"You didn't see anyone? No one else on the path to the overlook?"

"No one. The area was deserted." How many times did she have to tell him?

"This wasn't a drive of yours you forgot about?" he asked. "Maybe it fell out of your purse?"

"No." She shoved her chair back and stood, glaring down at him. "Why won't you believe me?"

"It's my job to be skeptical." He stood, also. A head taller and uncomfortably close. "I have to draw conclusions based on evidence not gut feelings."

Did that mean that in his gut he believed her? "Dane uses this kind of flash drive," she said, forcing herself to remain calm. "And this—" she indicated the screen "—is the type of report he analyzes every day."

"His daughter told us he gave these drives out to a lot of people," he said. "Maybe someone else who works at TDC, or a competitor, left the drive for you."

"Fine, if you want to think that. But why?"

Instead of answering, he reached into his other pocket and took out another evidence bag with another flash drive, this one blue, the WHW logo stamped across one side. "Where did you get that?" she asked.

"It was found this morning in the bed of Dane's pickup, wrapped in a TDC bandana."

"In his pickup? In the bottom of the canyon?"

He nodded. "I don't believe it was there yesterday," he said. "The bright yellow bandana stood out against the black truck, and I don't think I or the park ranger who assisted me would have overlooked it."

"Then do you believe me now—that Dane left these for us?"

"I believe someone left them," he said. "But I don't know yet who that was, or why."

"Maybe it was a cry for help," Cara said. "Or a clue as to what is going on. What's on that second drive?"

"I thought you and I could look at it and see."

That he had waited for her impressed her a little— but only a little. He had already admitted that he didn't understand the information on the first drive. She accepted the new drive and inserted it in a second port on the side of her laptop.

"It looks like more of the same," he said as letters and numbers filled the screen.

"It's a little different," she said. "This one is tracking water quality over time." She pointed to a graph at the right of the columns of figures. "It shows water quality worsening over time."

Jason regarded the screen again. "So what does it mean?"

She looked at the rows of numbers and letters. "It's a bad sample," she said. "Someone is really out of compliance."

"Where is it from?" he asked.

Cara shook her head. "Without a header, there's no way of knowing. It's the same for the first report. They give us some information, but not enough."

"What type of place then? If you had to guess."

"An old mine? A toxic waste dump? I really can't say."

"I thought all the mining around here was for gold and silver." This part of Colorado was pockmarked with abandoned mines dating from the late 1800s, most abandoned a hundred years ago.

"There's uranium, too," she said. "And they used arsenic and mercury to separate the precious metals from the worthless rock. All that stuff built up over the years and rain washes it down into streams and rivers." She studied the screen again. "TDC has some government contracts to clean up contaminated sites in the area. Maybe this is an initial analysis from one of those."

"Which brings us back to the question, why leave it for us to find?

"I don't know." She hit the button to print a copy of each report. "I'll compare this to files on Dane's computer at work and see if I come up with anything." She slipped both drives back into their evidence bags and handed them to him.

"I'll need a list of people Dane knew," Jason said. "Friends, romantic interests, coworkers. Anyone who might have insight into why he left and where he went."

Her spirits lifted. "Then you don't think he killed himself?"

He held up one hand. "At this point, we're not ruling out any possibility."

"But you haven't found a body."

He didn't answer. Instead he said. "Before, you told me the last time you saw Dane, he had a backpack."

"Yes. He was putting it into his truck. Did you find it?"

He hesitated and she wanted to shake him.

Finally he said, "It wasn't in the truck, or anywhere at the scene. An animal could have dragged it away."

"Or Dane has it." She stood, too agitated to sit still any longer. "But how did his truck end up at the bottom of the canyon? Did someone kidnap him and push the truck over the edge?"

"Why would someone kidnap him?" Jason asked. "And if he was kidnapped, how did he put the flash drive in your car?"

"Maybe he got away?" Dane stayed in shape and was tough.

"Then why not ask for help instead of leaving a meaningless portion of a report in your car and taking off again?"

"He must have had a reason," she said. Maybe it didn't make sense to someone who didn't know Dane. "He's one of the smartest people I know. And he's not impulsive. When he does something, he has a reason."

"Look, I want to help you," Jason said. "But you're not giving me much to work with. This doesn't look like a kidnapping to me. What's the motive? And where's the ransom demand?"

"Dane didn't kill himself," Cara said. "He wouldn't. If he wasn't kidnapped, then what's going on?"

"Maybe he ran away," Jason said.

"Ran away from what?"

He settled one hip on the corner of the table, a casual pose, though his expression remained guarded, focused on her. "Sometimes, people try to fake their own death in order to start over with a new identity somewhere else," he said. "Usually, it's because they want to escape debt or a bad relationship, or a crime they've committed."

"Dane wasn't in debt," she said. "He didn't have bad relationships and he's certainly not a criminal."

"Do you know that for sure?"

She hated the doubt that pinched at her. Dane was her boss, not her lover or even her best friend. She wasn't privy to his secrets. "I never saw anything to make me suspect trouble of any kind," she said.

"Get me that list of contacts," Jason said. "I'll see what I can find out."

"I'll type that up for you now." She sat in front of the laptop once more. While they had been talking, she had received two new work emails. On a Saturday? She frowned at the subject line on each—Re: Dane.

"What's wrong?" Jason moved in beside her.

She opened the first email.

From: M.Ruffino@TDCEnterprises.org
To: C.Mead@TDCEnterprises.org
Re: Dane
Cara, I you need to box up all of Dane's files and records. I want everything from his desk and office. Someone will be by at 9 sharp Monday morning to pick them up.
Mitchell Ruffino, VP of Operations
TDC Enterprises

Heart beating hard, she opened the second email.

From: M.Ruffino@TDCEnterprises.org
To: C.Mead@TDCEnterprises.org
Re: Dane
Keep this information strictly confidential.
Remember—I want everything.
MR

Cara glanced up at Jason. "I don't understand what this means," she said.

"Maybe it's standard procedure when an employee goes missing," he said.

She pulled out her phone and dialed the number for the TDC switchboard. Even though it was Saturday, it wasn't unusual for people to be there, putting in extra hours on projects in a time-crunch. She punched in the extension for the vice president's office, expecting to get his voice mail.

Instead, Ruffino himself answered. "Ruffino."

"Mr. Ruffino, this is Cara Mead. I received your

email about boxing up all of Dane's files. I don't understand. What's going on?"

"It's standard procedure when an employee is part of a criminal investigation," Ruffino said. "Everything in that office is now evidence."

She sagged back in her chair, the breath knocked out of her. It was several seconds before she could speak.

"Ms. Mead?" Ruffino asked.

She wet her lips and forced words from her throat. "How is Dane part of a criminal investigation?" she asked. "What's going on?"

"I'm afraid your boss is in serious trouble," Ruffino said. "We believe he's been embezzling money from the company for some time."

"Embezzlement?" The word sounded foreign on her tongue.

"That's right. He's stolen a considerable sum of money and we intend to prosecute to the fullest extent of the law. Now, you get all those files together for me. I want them ready by 9:00 a.m. sharp on Monday." Not waiting for an answer, he hung up.

Cara laid her phone on the table beside the laptop, stomach churning.

Jason put a hand on her shoulder. "Are you okay?" he asked. "What did he say?"

She looked up to meet his gaze and the concern in his eyes made hers burn with tears. "He said Dane stole a lot of money from TDC. But that can't be right. I'm sure it can't be right."

Chapter Six

At the entrance to TDC Enterprises, Cara punched in the code to silence the alarm with shaking hands, acutely aware of the security camera focused on her. Did anyone actually look at the footage from that camera? If anyone asked why she was at the office at six in the morning, she'd tell them she was anxious to have all of Dane's files and equipment boxed up and ready to go when whoever Mr. Ruffino was sending to retrieve them showed up at nine.

She crossed the small lobby to the elevator, the piped-in music that apparently played twenty-four hours a day sounding overly loud in the stillness. Alone in the elevator as it rose to the fifth floor of the building, she practiced taking deep, calming breaths, though her heart continued to pound and her stomach rolled with nausea.

This must be some huge mistake. Dane hadn't really stolen money from the company. Why would he? He made a six-figure salary and, unlike some of their co-workers, didn't live an extravagant lifestyle. He didn't take exotic vacations. His truck wasn't cheap, but it wasn't a Porsche, either. He lived in a modest home that had once been part of a ranch. His hobbies of hiking, fishing and volunteering with Welcome Home Warriors didn't take much money.

The police suspected he'd run away. And sending his truck into Black Canyon certainly looked like an attempt to fake his own death.

But that didn't explain the flash drive with the excerpt from a bad water quality report.

After the emails from Mitchell Ruffino, Jason hadn't said much. He'd listened to her protests that Dane wouldn't steal and promised to check into it, but doubt was written large in his expression. He probably saw all kinds of innocent-looking people do horrible things every day. Dane was just another criminal to him.

And she was just another woman who had trusted the wrong man.

She opened the door to the engineering department and flipped on the lights. After the subdued lighting of the elevator and hallway, the banks of bright LEDs made her wince. She hurried to her desk, right outside Dane's private corner office. As the chief environmental engineer for TDC, Dane ranked his own space. The other analysts and assistants worked in an open space crowded with desks and office machinery. Cara prayed none of them would decide to come in early this Monday morning.

She fished a key from an inside pocket of her purse and unlocked Dane's door. He'd presented her with the key last month, saying he might need her to access his office for him when he was working off-site. At the time, she'd been pleased with this gift—now she wondered if, even then, Dane was planning his escape.

She flipped on the lights and powered up the computer, then, while waiting for the machine to boot up, turned to the row of filing cabinets that filled one wall of the office.

The lateral files contained maps, architectural drawings and copies of deeds, surveys and historical documents related to the properties TDC had either developed or was thinking about developing. These included local projects such as a new elementary school not far from the park entrance, to abandoned mining sites the company was charged with cleaning up, to overseas office buildings and shopping malls. The firm of Terrell, Davis, and Compton had its fingers in pies all over the globe.

Dane's job focused primarily on environmental impact statements, soil analysis to determine the foundation type best suited for a property, and water analysis for potentially contaminated sites.

The computer screen glowed with a photo of a smiling Dane and his daughter, Audra. More than one visitor had mistaken the photo for one of Dane and his younger girlfriend or wife, an assumption that never pleased him. It didn't help that he looked younger than forty-one, with no gray in his thick brown hair, or that Audra, twenty-two, was the result of a brief relationship he'd had in college. Though he and Audra's mother had never married, Dane had developed a close relationship with his daughter over the years.

Cara fished a flash drive from her purse—not the

little red one Jason still had in evidence, but a slim silver one with the capacity to copy all of the files on Jason's computer. She inserted the little device into the USB port, typed in the command to copy, then returned to the filing cabinets.

Five minutes later, she was in front of the scanner, feeding in documents and sending them directly to her own laptop. She bounced one knee in agitation as she waited for the first pages to scan. What she was doing was strictly against company policy and maybe even illegal. She didn't know if an IT expert would be able to tell that she had copied Dane's files. She planned to attempt to wipe the scanner's memory when she was done with the hard copies, but didn't know how successful she would be.

She hadn't slept much the night before, worried about Dane—what he might have done and why, and where he might be now. She probably needed caffeine. Then again, the idea of coffee on her queasy stomach made her even queasier. And she didn't need anything more to hype her up. As it was, when the water cooler in the corner gurgled, she almost dropped the entire contents of a folder full of mining surveys.

She didn't even know why she was going to all this trouble. What was she planning to do with all this stuff she was copying? Last night, as she had lain awake, unable to sleep, she'd hatched a plan to go through all of Dane's data to figure out what the information on the flash drives meant. He had left that first drive in her car for a reason. It was a clue as to why he had disappeared and, right now, at least, it seemed she was the only person who cared enough to figure it out.

Standing in Dane's empty office with the light glaring and the scanner whirring, Cara just felt foolish. But she fed the next document into the scanner, feeling she had stepped too far over the line to stop now.

As THE SUN rose over the peaks to the east of Black Canyon of the Gunnison on Monday morning, Jason set barricades to close off the Dragon Point overlook. A quarter mile farther up the road, park employees were closing access to this stretch of the South Rim Road. Tourists would be disappointed not to be able to admire and photograph some of the park's most iconic views, but the park service needed to get Dane's truck out of the canyon without the distraction of onlookers.

The wrecker, a 50-ton unit from Grand Junction with a specialized boom, backed toward the canyon rim, easing between boulders, warning beeper blaring, sun spotlighting the gleaming red sides. The driver stopped well back from the edge, left the truck running and he and the vehicle's two passengers climbed out.

They joined Jason at the rim. "I don't see the truck," the younger, shorter man with a bushy beard said.

"It's down there," Jason said. "It's black and in the shadows." The depth and narrowness of the canyon meant the wreck was in shadow most of the time.

"Take a portable spotlight with you," the driver told the bearded man. "And don't forget your safety gear. The last thing I want is to have to haul your carcass out of there."

The young man nodded and returned to the truck to don a bright yellow-and-orange reflective vest and hard hat. Then he shouldered a backpack, switched on a headlamp and started toward the trail leading into the canyon. Jason had no desire to make the hike down into the canyon a third time, but he felt a twinge of concern. That trail wasn't for amateurs, especially in the dark. "Has he ever made that hike before?" he asked.

"Rob's idea of a good time is free-climbing stupid sick cliffs," the third man, ruddy-faced and clean-shaven, said. "He's been looking forward to this."

"While he's headed down there, we'll get the boom ready," the driver, a paunchy man in his fifties, said.

While the two men worked extending the boom in sections, setting up outriggers to balance the rig, and hooking up cables, Jason let his mind wander. Was Dane Trask out there somewhere in the darkness? Or was he on his way to Tahiti or some other exotic locale, his new life funded by money he'd stolen from his employer?

Cara hadn't said much after she'd spoken to Ruffino, only that she couldn't believe Dane would do something like that. Jason wanted to do his own follow-up on the criminal investigation the TDC vice president had mentioned, but he was stuck at the overlook until the wrecker had done its job, without cell service or internet.

The driver came to stand beside him, watching as the other man operated the remote control for the boom. "Do you do this sort of thing much?" Jason asked.

"Similar. Usually it's a truck driver who's gone over

the edge on a mountain pass. But there have been a handful of suicides."

"We haven't confirmed this is a suicide."

The driver spat a stream of tobacco juice. "You don't think someone accidentally drove off that cliff, do you?"

Jason didn't bother with a response.

An hour later, he caught the glimmer of a light signaling from the bottom of the canyon. The driver returned to his truck and a few moments later called out, "We're ready!"

The groan and squeal of cables and the scrape of metal on rock made Jason's teeth hurt. The noise grew louder and he regretted not thinking to bring earplugs. The wrecker driver and his helper, he noticed, both wore ear protection.

Inch by inch, the mangled pickup rose out of the canyon. As it hung in the air, it looked even more pathetic than it had on the rocks below, like a child's toy someone had stepped on. "What happened to the driver?" the boom operator asked over the din.

"We haven't found him yet," Jason said.

The operator shook his head. "I'll bet he didn't walk away from that one."

The mangled truck reached the rim of the canyon and the ruddy-faced operator guided it over the rocks. Then he ran forward to help the driver with the cables.

A horn tap made Jason look around in time to see a Ranger cruiser ease past the road barricades. The vehicle parked and Hud got out. "How's it going?" he asked when he joined Jason at the edge of the canyon.

"These guys did a great job," Jason said. "I'll talk to

the operator in the canyon when he gets back up here, see if he spotted anything unusual, but I'm not expecting much."

"Yeah, well…we've had a new development I thought you'd want to know about."

Jason tensed. "What is it?"

"You were right that it was blood on that bandana. Human, and type A positive. Dane Trask's blood type."

By THE TIME the first employees began filtering in at eight thirty on Monday morning, Cara was about to pack away the last of the documents and seal the last of the boxes. Her best work friend, Maisie, found her in Dane's office, stacks of cardboard banker's boxes surrounding her.

"Uh-oh." Maisie's eyes widened as she assessed the situation. She moved closer, lowering her voice. "Did Dane get fired? Is that why he hasn't been around the past few days?"

Cara shook her head. "All I know is I got an email from Mr. Ruffino on Saturday, telling me to box up all of Dane's stuff."

"Mr. Ruffino himself emailed you?"

"I know, right?" Cara said. She didn't remember the vice president of operations ever speaking to her. She was a little surprised that he even knew how to contact her, though she supposed that was the sort of thing a VP should know. Though Misters Terrell, Davis and Compton had visited during the new building's grand opening, for the employees that worked at the company's headquarters, Mitchell Ruffino was the man who ran the show.

Maisie frowned at the growing stack of boxes. "What's going on?" she asked. "Have you heard from Dane?"

Cara shook her head and added a stack of files to the box. "No, and I'm worried about him."

"If he's gone, are you going to work for the new chief engineer?" Maisie asked.

"I don't know," Cara said. She hadn't even considered what might happen to her if Dane truly was no longer employed by TDC.

Maisie gave her a sympathetic look and squeezed her arm. "Whatever happens, you'll make it through. You'll do a good job no matter where you end up."

"Thanks." She sealed the lid on the box and reached for another.

"Can I do anything to help?" Maisie asked.

"Thanks, but this is the last box."

Just then, two men in gray suits appeared in the doorway. "Caroline Mead?" one asked.

Behind Cara, Maisie made a squeaking noise then slipped by her, past the two men and out the door.

Cara didn't blame Maisie for making herself scarce. The expensive-looking gray suits were the only thing that looked corporate about these two, who had matching shaved heads and muscles. The only difference between them was that one was African American and the other was white. They looked like a matched set of bodyguards, all hard lines and muscular planes.

"I'm Caroline Mead," she said.

The white man fixed her with a cold-water stare that chilled her through. "We're here for Mr. Trask's things," he said.

She took a deep breath, fighting for calm. "This is everything," she said, indicating the boxes stacked around her. "The laptop is in that bag."

The guy opened a desk drawer. It was empty. Cara had cleared out the contents of every one. She had even boxed up the spare jacket and gym clothes from the closet in the corner.

The black guy hefted two of the heavy boxes, while the white guy took the laptop and another box. They were almost to the door when their exit was blocked by a third man.

"I'll have to ask you to put those back" said a voice that made Cara weak at the knees. She grabbed the side of the desk for support and tried to see around the broad back of the white guy.

"Officer Beck, is that you?"

Chapter Seven

The distress in Cara's voice made Jason clench his free hand into a fist. Had these two suits been bullying or intimidating her? "Officer Beck and Lieutenant Dance, Ranger Brigade." He thrust the warrant in his other hand toward the black man. "These files are evidence in an ongoing case and we'll be taking them into custody."

The man looked as if he wanted to argue. His knuckles paled where he gripped the file boxes.

Lieutenant Michael Dance stepped in closer behind Jason, his broad-shouldered form effectively blocking the doorway.

"We were told to deliver these to Mr. Ruffino." The white guy set his burden on the desk behind Cara and shifted enough that Jason thought he caught a glimpse of a shoulder holster. Since when did office workers go around armed?

"Keep your hands where I can see them and move into the outer office, please," he said. He stepped back to allow the two men to pass. Dance moved out of the way, also, one hand resting not-so-casually on the butt of his service revolver. Jason guessed these two set Dance on edge as much as they did him.

"What's the meaning of this?" the white guy blustered, turning back to Jason. "Everything in those boxes is the property of TDC Enterprises. You can't just barge in here and seize it."

"That warrant says we can," Jason said, aware that all semblance of work in the outer office had ceased and half a dozen men and women at the various desks around the room were watching the drama play out. He glanced to his right, to where Cara remained frozen in front of the desk. "We're investigating the disappearance of Dane Trask. We believe items in those boxes may help reveal his whereabouts."

The black man held up both hands. "I need to call Mr. Ruffino to let him know what's going on," he said. "I need to get my phone."

"Go ahead," Jason said.

With exaggerated slowness, the man took a cell phone from the inside pocket of his suit jacket and punched in a number. "Mr. Ruffino, this is Durrell. There are two cops here with a warrant authorizing them to take the contents of Dane Trask's office into evidence for a case they're working on."

Durrell listened for a moment, nodding, then thrust the phone toward Jason. "He wants to speak with you."

"Who are you and what organization are you with?" a man's slightly nasal voice demanded as Jason put the phone to his ear.

"Officer Jason Beck, Ranger Brigade."

"The Ranger— Oh, that outfit based in the national park."

"That's correct," Jason said. "Who are you and what organization are you with?"

"I'm Mitchell Ruffino, vice president in charge of operations for TDC. What could Dane Trask possibly have to do with Black Canyon National Park?"

"His truck was found yesterday in the bottom of the canyon, having plummeted off one of the overlooks," Jason said. "This was after he was reported missing."

"Who reported him missing?" Ruffino demanded, sounding as if he intended to find and punish that person.

Jason glanced at Cara again. She was leaning forward, a look of intense concentration on her delicate features.

"I don't think that's relevant," Jason said. "But we're investigating Mr. Trask's disappearance and the contents of his office could contain vital evidence."

"I can tell you why Trask disappeared," Ruffino said. "He skipped out because he embezzled a hundred thousand dollars from this company and knew he was on the verge of being caught. Those files are vital to recovering our stolen money."

"As part of my investigation, I contacted other area law enforcement agencies and none of them reported charges being filed or accusations of embezzlement being levied against Mr. Trask."

Silence greeted his words and, for a moment, Jason wondered if Ruffino had hung up, perhaps to storm to this office and confront him in person. Finally, the executive said, "You must understand that organizations such as ours prefer to conduct our own internal investigation into the matter before we turn things over to the police."

"You can certainly do that," Jason said. "Meanwhile, until our investigation is complete, we're taking custody of these items. They will be returned to you when we no longer need them."

"I'll need to see that warrant," Ruffino said.

"Of course. Mr. Durrell can bring it to you now."

Ruffino did hang up on him then. Jason handed the warrant to Durrell. "Mr. Ruffino wants to see that now," he said.

Durrell took the paper, then glanced at his partner. With a last glare at the two cops, the men left the office.

Jason and Dance moved farther into the office. Dance shut the door behind them. Cara leaned against the desk, her face pale. "What's going on?" she asked.

"After I left you yesterday, I made some phone calls," Jason said. "I discovered TDC hadn't filed any charges of embezzlement or theft or anything else against Dane Trask."

"Corporations often like to hush up that sort of thing," she said.

"Your missing person's report and the discovery of Dane's truck were enough for me to get authorization to take a look at his bank accounts. If he was embezzling tens of thousands of dollars, none of it was getting anywhere near his personal accounts. And he hasn't used his credit cards or his cell phone since you saw him last. Someone trying to fake his own death would know enough to avoid those two things, but it takes a lot of money to start life over someplace new and I didn't find anything showing Trask had stashed away funds." He put his hand on the topmost box. "I need to dig deeper, and for that, we need these files."

She nodded, looking relieved.

"I'll see about getting a dolly to carry these out," Dance said, and left them.

When he was gone, Jason moved closer to Cara. "Are you okay?" he asked.

She nodded. "Yeah. It's been a tough morning."

"Who were those two?" he asked. "The guys who came to collect the boxes?"

"I've never seen them before in my life." She rubbed her arms, as if trying to warm herself. "They looked tough."

"They looked like bodyguards," Jason said. "Why would Ruffino need that kind of muscle?"

She blew out a breath. "I don't know, but I feel a lot better, knowing you'll have the files instead of them." Her eyes met his. "I know it looks bad, Dane disappearing, and then these accusations about embezzlement coming out, but I can't believe they're true. He just wasn't—he isn't—that kind of man."

"Some criminals are very good at fooling people," he said.

She lifted her chin. "I know that. I'm not as naive as I look. But Dane isn't a criminal. I don't know what's going on, but I'm going to try to find out."

"You need to leave the investigating to us," he said.

Her gaze remained steady, considering. "You've already done more than I expected," she said. "I thought you believed I was making the whole thing up."

He had believed that, at least at first. But spending time with her yesterday, he had detected no deception in her story, and her loyalty to her boss had touched him. What would it be like to have another person believe in him so fiercely?

And the memory of that pickup, smashed at the bottom of the canyon, had stayed with him. If Dane Trask had sent that vehicle over the edge himself, it was the act of a desperate man. Jason wanted to know what was behind that desperation.

The door opened and Jason took a step back, putting a little distance between himself and Cara. Dance wheeled in a dolly. "Any suggestions where we should look first?" Jason asked Cara.

"The computer," she said. "Anything Dane is working on is there." She pressed her lips together, as if tempted to say more.

"Anything else we should know?" he asked.

She shook her head, avoiding his gaze now. Disappointment clawed at him. She was being evasive, either lying or holding something back.

Some people had an instinctive distrust of the law. Other people feared anyone with a badge or shied away out of guilt.

Solving this case would be much easier if he could get Cara to trust him. But he sensed she wasn't one to let down her guard easily. She was going to make him work for any bit of trust he might get.

"WHAT WAS ALL that about?"

Maisie didn't waste any time cornering Cara after Jason and his partner had left the office, taking all of Dane's work with them. Eyes shining with curiosity, she leaned over Cara's desk, her voice just above a whisper. "Is Dane really being investigated? Did he really steal from the company? And where is he now?"

"I don't know the answer to any of those questions," Cara said. Which wasn't a lie. The whole exchange this morning had left her sad and confused. On the one hand, Jason seemed to believe that Dane was missing and possibly in trouble. On the other hand, it certainly looked like Dane could be guilty of something.

"Well, come on. Dane was your boss. You must know something."

Cara shook her head. "I don't know anything, really."

Maisie blew out a breath, stirring her long brown bangs. "Well, at least the cops were hot. And who were the two suits? Great bodies, but kind of scary-looking."

"I've never seen them before," Cara said.

"Me neither, but if they work here now, I need to find out where." Maisie grinned. "A little scary could be exciting, you know?"

Cara would take safe and calm over scary and exciting any day, but merely gave her friend a weak smile. "I'll let you know if I find out anything else."

Maisie returned to work and Cara tried to focus on formatting a report Dane had sent to her right before he'd walked out of the office with his backpack. She paid close attention to its contents, hoping he had left her some clue as to what he was up to. But the report—

a summary of the water and soil analysis at the site of a potential office complex TDC planned to build in Nevada—was routine and boring. "All preliminary tests show the site well-suited for the project as outlined," Dane had concluded.

Every time the door to the office opened or someone approached Cara's desk, she braced herself, expecting Mr. Ruffino to summon her and grill her about Dane and everything that had happened. But nothing happened.

At five o'clock, she headed home, the flash drive with Dane's files buried deep in her purse. Though Jason had said he intended to search the documents for clues about what might have happened to Dane, Cara believed she was better equipped to see the significance of the information.

At least she owed it to Dane to try.

Two blocks from her home, she pulled up to a stop sign and glanced in the rearview mirror. Two cars back, a black SUV with dark windows idled. She stared at the vehicle. Hadn't she seen it as she'd turned off the road that led from TDC headquarters? It had been parked on the side of the road. She had registered its presence, but otherwise not thought much about it.

She made a left turn and the SUV turned, also. Impulsively, she swung right onto the next street. The SUV cruised past and she breathed a sigh of relief. The morning's ordeal and her own guilt over copying Dane's files were obviously making her paranoid.

She made her way home down a series of back streets. Once she thought she saw the black SUV waiting at an intersection ahead, but the driver signaled a turn in the direction opposite the one she was traveling. She gripped the steering wheel tightly and told herself she was being silly.

Still, relief flooded her when she reached her home, the small cottage with its steeply pitched green-metal roof and delicate wooden gingerbread outlining the broad front porch a welcome sanctuary from the stresses of the day.

Inside the house, she changed into yoga pants and a T-shirt, fixed a sandwich and a glass of iced tea, and sat at the kitchen table with her laptop. She downloaded the documents she had scanned in that morning, then inserted the flash drive with all the files from Dane's computer and studied the file listing.

Dane had worked for TDC for six years and many of the files dated back to those early days. She decided to focus on the most recent data, in the hope that something Dane had written about or marked would provide a clue as to his current situation and whereabouts.

She determined that in the two weeks prior to his disappearance, Dane had been working primarily on analyzing water samples from three sites—the property in Nevada slated for the new office building, a Superfund cleanup of an old mine near Black Canyon, and the new elementary school, also nearby. She studied the columns of numbers and abbreviations. She didn't have Dane's scientific background, but she thought she was sharp enough to spot any big discrepancies.

But after an hour, her head ached and she had found

nothing in the reports for the three properties that raised alarms.

She got up to stretch her legs and refill her tea glass. The sun had set and dusk was fast turning to dark, so she moved to the front window to pull shut the drapes. The street was silent, the trees, parked cars and shrubbery in front of neighboring houses reduced to black smudges against gray shadows. Everything looked normal, yet it didn't feel that way. She couldn't shake this edginess that made her skin crawl—as if she was being watched.

She jerked the drapes shut, checked that the locks on the front and back doors were secure, and told herself to snap out of it. Then her cell phone rang, the country ballad she'd chosen as her ringtone sounding overly loud in the stillness.

She hurried to the reclaim the phone from where it danced on the kitchen table, vibrating and ringing. She didn't recognize the number on the screen, so she answered cautiously, prepared to hang up on an automated sales call. "Cara? It's Officer Beck. How are you doing?"

"Hi. Uh, I'm okay, I guess." She lowered herself into the kitchen chair. The last person she'd expected to hear from was Jason Beck. "Did you find something useful in Dane's files?"

"Not yet. I just wanted to check in because you looked pretty shaken when I left this morning."

"Yes, I was shaken. I had two thugs and then two cops in the office."

"Hey, cops aren't so bad." His tone was teasing.

"Maybe *you're* not so bad. I can't say the same about others I've met."

"Hmm. Something tells me there's a story behind that statement. Some day I want to hear it."

Cara remained silent. She could count on the fingers of one hand the number of people who knew about her brother. Nothing like bringing up a murdered sibling to put a damper on a conversation.

She gave Jason credit for being able to take a hint. "What happened after I left TDC this morning?" he asked.

"Nothing," she said. "I mean, people talked about Dane, but no one really knew anything. Then everyone went back to work."

"Ruffino didn't grill you?"

"Why would he?" she said. "I'm just another cog in the wheel to people like him."

"I spoke to the sheriff's office," Jason said. "Dane's daughter, Audra, filed a missing person's report with them a few days ago. We encouraged her to do so."

"They wouldn't listen to me when I talked to them," she said.

"Sometimes they pay more attention to family."

"So what happens now?" she asked. "Do you turn the search for Dane over to the local sheriff?"

"No, we have priority, especially since Dane's truck was found in the canyon. But Audra's report formalizes everything and maybe frees up some resources. I'm still trying to arrange for a plane or a helicopter to do an aerial search."

"I wish there was more that I could do," she said.

"When you were packing up Dane's things this morning, did you have a chance to look through much?" Jason asked. "Did you see anything that struck you as odd or different?"

"Not really." She bit her lip, resisting the impulse to confess that she had made copies of all of Dane's records. That probably qualified as theft of company property or something, and he didn't need to know. "You'll let me know if you find anything, won't you?" she asked.

"I'll keep you as informed as I can."

What does that mean exactly? She started to ask as much when a scraping sound on her front porch made her almost drop the phone. She knew that sound—it was the noise she made every time she returned home after dark and discovered she'd forgotten to leave the porch light on. Invariably, she ended up banging her shin on the cast-iron planter of petunias. The combination of the planter scraping on the wooden porch floor and muttered cursing was unmistakable.

"Cara? Are you still there?"

"I'm still here," she whispered. She tiptoed toward the front door and pressed her eye to the peephole. Was she imagining that darker shadow next to the porch post?

"What's wrong?" Jason asked. "I can hardly hear you."

She moved away from the door, all the way into the kitchen. She grabbed the largest knife from the magnetic bar by the stove. The problem with a weapon like that was that she'd have to get really close to use it.

"Cara?" Jason's voice was louder now.

She pressed the phone tight against her ear. "There's someone on my front porch," she said softly. "Someone who shouldn't be there."

"Lock yourself in your bedroom. I'm calling 9-1-1 and I'm on my way."

Chapter Eight

Jason skidded around the curves on the rough mountain road from his rented cabin to the highway into town. Headlights on bright, he scanned the roadside for deer or elk that might decide to leap into his path, and listened to the chatter on the police radio for any word that the Montrose police had apprehended Cara's intruder.

With the locals on the way, Cara didn't need him to run to her rescue. She probably didn't want him. But he was going anyway, compelled by a mixture of curiosity and protectiveness and attraction. Something about her drew him. She was a puzzle he needed to figure out, almost as much as he needed to solve the puzzle of Dane Trask's disappearance.

On the surface, the story looked straightforward. A man is stealing money from his employer. He finds out he's on the verge of getting caught, so he fakes his own death and skips town.

But something about TDC's insistence on that narrative didn't ring true to Jason. The company's haste to confiscate Dane's computer and files wasn't normal operating procedure in his experience. Throw in two beefy guys in charge of retrieving the files, and every instinct told him he needed to look a lot closer at all of this.

He reached Cara's neighborhood and turned onto her street. Her house was dark, with no sign of the local cops or of an intruder. Jason drove past the house, parked around the corner and walked back, moving as soundlessly as possible and keeping to the shadows.

The house was a square two-story cottage, with a steeply sloped metal roof, windows flanked by wooden shutters, and a covered porch across the front. Secluded in the shadow of a massive lilac bush, he studied the scene and froze as something moved on the porch. Something large and bulky, just below a large window.

He drew his service weapon, a Glock 22, and a large flashlight and approached the porch. When he was standing directly opposite the bulky figure, he raised the gun and switched on the flashlight. "This is the police!" he shouted. "Stop and put your hands where I can see them."

The figure—a man dressed all in black, including a black ski mask pulled down to obscure his face— shielded his eyes from the glare of the light with one upraised arm. He thrust the other in front of him and barreled forward, almost knocking Jason off his feet. The gun fired, the bullet well off course, thudding harmlessly into the dirt.

Jason holstered the weapon and raced after the man, but big as he was, the guy had speed. By the time Jason reached the end of the block, the man was gone.

Jason retraced his steps to the house. Lights were on inside now, as well as in all the houses around Cara's.

Nothing like a gunshot in the middle of an otherwise peaceful night to rouse people from their beds.

A Montrose Police Department black-and-white pulled to the curb as Jason approached. He held up his hands. "I'm the Ranger Brigade officer who called this in," he said.

The local cop climbed out of the patrol car and approached. He was young, fit and looking a little uncertain. "We got a report of an intruder," he said after he had examined Jason's ID and returned it to him. "Have you seen anything?"

"He was on the front porch." Jason motioned toward the house. "He was trying to force the window. You might want to take a look at it in a minute. Meanwhile, he ran that way." He pointed down the street.

The officer glanced down the street then reached for his shoulder mic. "Do you have a description of the suspect?" he asked.

"He was big, beefy and dressed all in black," Jason said. "He was wearing a ski mask and gloves." He turned to start up the walk.

"Sir, where are you going?" the young cop asked.

"I'm going to check on the woman inside the house."

The young cop didn't say anything. It wouldn't have mattered to Jason if he had. He didn't want to wait any longer to find out if Cara was okay.

He rang the bell then knocked. "Cara, it's me, Jason."

The door swung open and Cara, barefoot and wearing yoga pants and a loose T-shirt, stared at him, a large knife in her right hand. "What's going on?" she asked. "Did you catch him?"

"He ran away," Jason said. "I think it's safe to put the knife away now."

She stared at the knife, as if trying to remember why she was holding it. She set it on a small table by the door then stepped back and held the door open wider. "You'd better come in."

His first thought upon entering the house was that it smelled like her—warm and spicy with a touch of sweetness. He hadn't really noticed this when he'd stopped by with the flash drive the other night. Next, he took in the framed photographs, books and plants that filled this front room. It wasn't an unpleasant clutter, but a homey one. All these personal items pointed to someone who was making a home in this space, not just biding time until something better came along.

"This is a great house," he said.

"Thanks. It was a dump when I bought it, but it's coming along. I did most of the work myself." He didn't miss the note of pride behind the words.

"You did a great job." He ran his hand along the smooth wood of a built-in sideboard as she hugged her arms across her body. Was she cold or merely defensive?

"Are you okay?" he asked when they had passed through the living room into the kitchen.

"A little scared." She rubbed her shoulders as if to ward off a chill. "And a lot angry. How dare someone try to break into my home? Did you see him?"

"Yes. He was crouching under that window." He nodded toward the big window to the right of the front door. "He was dressed all in black, with a ski mask, so I can't tell you who he was, or even much about his appearance."

"All the windows and doors have good locks, but maybe I need an alarm system, too." She leaned back against the counter, arms crossed over her chest. "This is supposed to be a safe neighborhood. I haven't heard of anyone else having a break-in."

Jason took up position beside her—close, but not touching. His first instinct was to comfort her and to tell her not to worry. But his law enforcement training vetoed that approach. "Is it possible this attempted break-in is connected to Dane's disappearance?" he asked.

Her face paled and she hugged herself even more tightly. "Why do you say that?"

"I've never met Dane Trask. Is it possible he was trying to break in?"

"Dane wouldn't have to break into my house. All he would have to do is knock and I'd let him in."

"What does Dane look like?" Jason asked. He'd seen the ID photos of the man, but they didn't show much.

"He's about six feet tall, slender build, dark hair cut short, blue eyes."

"The guy who was trying to break in was bigger than that," Jason said. "Bulkier, and a little shorter, I think."

"Dane wouldn't break in, and he wouldn't frighten me this way."

"All right, then let's look at this from another angle. Maybe whoever was trying to get in here wants something you have or something you know."

Pink bloomed on her pale cheeks. "Why would anyone think I have or know anything?" she asked, avoiding his gaze.

He moved to stand in front of her. When she didn't raise her eyes to his, he gently nudged her chin until her eyes met his. "Did you turn over all of Dane's records this morning?" he asked. "Or did you keep something back? Maybe something you didn't think was important?"

"I turned over everything," she said, lowering her gaze. Her expression grew troubled. "But I made copies of everything before I did."

"Why did you do that? Were you afraid data might be compromised or lost?"

"I wanted to look through everything to see if I could figure out what Dane was working on before he left."

"What did you find out?"

"He had three jobs he was involved in—an office complex in Nevada, a Superfund mine cleanup in the mountains near here, and the new elementary school near the national park." She shook her head. "Nothing looked out of the ordinary."

"Did anything match the fragment of the report on the drive that was left in your car?" he asked.

"No. But if someone was trying to break into my home because they're afraid I'll find something in those files, then I'm more determined than ever to keep looking. And don't waste your breath telling me I shouldn't get involved. I'm already involved and I'm a lot more likely to spot something off about those reports than you are."

Her eyes met his and what he saw there sent a thrill

through him—not fear, but fierceness, a determination to keep going over his and anyone else's objections.

Her gaze shifted from his eyes to his lips and awareness crackled between them. He put a hand on her arm and she leaned into the touch, leaned into him, her face tilted to his, her eyes half closed, her breathing quick and shallow.

He caressed her upper arms and angled his head toward hers, blood rushing, heart racing—

The doorbell jolted them apart. Cara gaped at him, dazed, then rushed from the room.

He hurried after her. She checked the security peephole then opened the door to the young officer Jason had spoken to earlier and an older, female officer with very short blond hair. "Did you catch the person who was trying to break into my house?" Cara asked.

"No, ma'am," the younger officer said. "But we're still looking for him. Are you missing any personal items?"

"No. He didn't succeed in breaking in," she said.

The female officer turned to Jason. "Would you recognize the man if you saw him again?" she asked.

"Probably not," he said. "He was wearing a ski mask and gloves."

"There are some tool marks around the window frame, but you must have scared him off before he got very far," the younger officer said.

Some of the color had leached from Cara's face again. "What if he comes back?" she asked.

"Call 9-1-1 and we'll have someone here right away," the woman said. She gave Cara her card and the two left.

Cara sat on the sofa in the darkened room. "I don't know how I'll sleep, worried whoever that was will come back."

"You could go to a hotel," he said.

"I can't live in a hotel." She sat straighter. "And it makes me angry all over again that this creep might run me out of my home." She looked toward the door. "I'll just sit up all night, and tomorrow I'll call the alarm company."

"Don't you have to work tomorrow?" he asked.

"If I still have a job." She shrugged. "Without Dane there, I'm having to work to look busy. Once someone in payroll or accounting or human resources realizes they're paying me to do nothing, I'll be out the door in no time."

Jason could have made a smart remark about executives being paid millions to do nothing, but thought better of it. "If you're going to sit up all night worrying, I'll sit with you," he said.

"You don't have to do that!"

But if he didn't, he'd probably lie awake in his own bed, worrying about her. "We can take a look at those files you copied. Maybe both of us working together will spot something."

She smiled, and the force of the look rocked him back on his heels. It wasn't the kiss he had wanted earlier, but it was something.

CARA MADE COFFEE and brought two cups to the table. The caffeine probably wouldn't improve her jitteriness, but she hoped it would sharpen her focus. If she was going to help Dane, she needed answers.

She sat and pulled her chair up closer to the table. Jason positioned his chair beside her. She caught the scent of him—starch and soap and clean man—and a tremor raced across her nerves. Sitting there with him, the world silent and dark around them, felt so intimate. When he'd run his hand along the sideboard, a shiver had raced through her, as if he was touching her with such tenderness.

She shook off the thought. It had been a long time since she'd been this close to anyone. After Corey's death, she had felt so fragile for so long. Relationships took energy she didn't have to give.

"Tell me more about Dane," Jason said. "He must have been a pretty great boss for you to go to so much trouble to help him now."

"He is a great boss." She refused to speak of Dane in the past tense. "He's a good person." How could she explain this so that Jason would see that Dane wasn't the type of person who would steal anything, much less a hundred thousand dollars? "Dane paid the electric bill for one of the building custodians who was about to get his power cut off. He didn't make a big deal about it or say anything, he just went down to the power company and paid the bill. I only found out about it by accident. He helped people like that all the time—veterans especially, but other people, too."

"Did he help you?" Jason asked. "Is that why you're so loyal to him?"

She felt shaky again, unnerved that this man could

read her so clearly. "You don't miss much, do you?" She took a sip of her coffee, not even tasting it. "When my brother died, Dane insisted on buying a ticket for me to fly back to Houston to be with my family. I had to stay longer than I was entitled to for bereavement leave, but he pulled strings somehow and made sure I got paid during the extra time off."

"That's a great boss, all right," Jason said.

"It wasn't the money that mattered most," she said. "When I got back after the funeral, he didn't try to pretend nothing had happened. He talked to me. He asked me about my brother, and he didn't get upset when I cried. Talking to him made things easier."

"I'm sorry to hear about your brother," he said. "What was his name?"

The nervousness she had been fighting melted away with that question. Most people's first reaction was "How did he die?" or "When did he die?" But Dane had asked for his name first.

"His name was Corey. He was two years younger than me, and we were pretty close." She took a deep breath. "He was murdered."

Jason stiffened but didn't recoil. "That's tough," he said. "Really tough. I'd like to hear what happened—if you want to tell me."

"Corey had a problem…" She began as she always did. "With heroin and prescription painkillers. He'd tried to kick the addiction a few times—even did a stint in rehab once. But he kept going back. When my parents called to tell me he'd died, I was sure they'd say it was an overdose. But he'd been shot." She swallowed. "Three times."

Jason's hand covered hers. He didn't speak, but the warm pressure of his hand on hers said volumes. "Did they find his killer?" he asked after a moment.

"No."

He withdrew his hand and leaned back, putting distance between them. "Is that why you don't like cops?" he asked.

"I don't dislike cops," she said. She didn't dislike him. "But I don't trust them. The ones assigned to my brother's case didn't seem to think he was worth their time." The memory still hurt and she had to look away. "Dane offered to pay for a private detective to investigate, but I couldn't let him do that."

"I'm sorry you had to go through that," he said. "And I'm glad Dane did what he could to make it easier on you."

She liked that he didn't try to defend the Houston cops. And maybe he saw Dane in a more favorable light now.

She pushed the half cup of cooling coffee away. "I can't do anything for my brother, but I can try to help Dane. I thought we could compare all the water quality reports from the three jobs he's working on with the fragment of the report on the flash drive I think he left for me to see if we can find a match."

"Is it possible his disappearance has nothing to do with his work?" Jason asked.

"Anything is possible," she said. "But he never mentioned any trouble in his personal life."

"His daughter said he didn't have a girlfriend. Not a current one, anyway."

"I know he dated women from time to time, but his last serious relationship ended six months ago. He was still friends with the woman."

"Is that Eve Shea? Audra mentioned her, too."

"Yes, Eve. They dated several years before they broke it off."

"Why did they break up? You said something about it before, but I can't remember."

"I think she wanted to get married and have children. Dane's daughter, Audra, was grown, and he always said he didn't want more children."

"And he got along well with the daughter?"

"Yes. They were close. And before you ask, she didn't have any trouble in her life, either. She's a smart young woman, financially and emotionally stable. Dane always said he never worried about her, she had such a good head on her shoulders."

"How about Audra's mother?"

"She was a brief relationship he had in college. She's married to an ophthalmologist and lives in Kansas City. She and Dane weren't close, but they got along well. She always invites Dane to anything that involves Audra—birthday parties and that sort of thing. I never sensed any animosity there."

"All right, we'll focus on the job," Jason said. "I just don't want to be shortsighted and miss any other possibilities."

She nodded and pulled up the first file. Jason was rising higher in her estimation by the moment. But talk was cheap. His actions would count more with her.

Chapter Nine

Jason tried to focus on the columns of numbers and letters on the computer screen, but his sleep-deprived brain insisted on shifting his attention to the soft curve of Cara's neck, or the floral scent of her hair. He was lost in a fantasy that involved kissing her neck and threading his fingers through her hair when the sound of his name recalled his attention.

"You're not listening, are you?" Cara asked. She had bluish smudges under each eye and looked exhausted.

"I'm sorry, no." He wiped a hand over his face, as if that would somehow wake him up. The clock in the lower right-hand corner of the computer screen read 3:11 a.m. "I'm not really a numbers guy."

She sat back. "We're not finding anything, anyway. Do you want to try to get some sleep? I can't promise my sofa is that comfortable, but you're welcome to it."

He shook his head. "Not yet." He was too wired from all the coffee he had consumed over the last few hours. "Let's just talk. Tell me how you ended up in your job."

"I have a degree in business. I don't want to be anyone's boss, but I'm good with details. TDC is a good company to work for."

It sounded boring to him, but she didn't sound unhappy with the work.

"What about you?" she asked. "How did you end up as a cop?"

"I did a year in the Peace Corps after college," he said. "Then I got a job working with teens in an Outward Bound type project. I like being outdoors, so I decided to become a park ranger. I was drawn to the law enforcement aspect of the job and eventually the National Parks police. And now I'm here."

"Wow," she said when he finished. "I bet that's not the usual career path."

"You might be surprised. All kinds of people work in law enforcement."

"Maybe you're different because you were a park ranger first," she said. "I can't imagine you've had to deal with too many seamy crimes to make you jaded."

"As a park ranger you deal with people," Jason said. "Some of them aren't so nice. Some of them believe they can get away with more in a wilderness setting." He'd had to deal with murder, rape, kidnapping and a host of lesser crimes. The fact that these wrongdoings took place in otherwise idyllic settings sometimes made them seem even more horrific.

Cara turned her attention back to the documents on the computer screen, so he did, as well, reading again the notes about turbidity and parts per million of arsenic and mercury. At the bottom of the report a section described the appearance of the water, whether or not it was cloudy or clear, silty, muddy, green with algae, et cetera. She pointed to a single word in the description box: *bloody.* "Look at that."

Jason's eyebrows lifted. "He's saying there's blood in the water?"

She shook her head. "No, I remember this. There was a lot of iron in the water, and suspended minerals, so that it was very red and thick. Like ketchup. Or blood. Dane wrote that in the original report and we joked about freaking out the engineers who explain these reports to clients. Sure enough, someone higher up kicked it back and he had to change it to something like 'red from high mineral content.'" Her fingers flew over the keys, searching for a different file. "But now I know where this fragment of a report is from."

She found the file she wanted and pulled it up in split screen alongside the information from the first flash drive. "These are reports from the Mary Lee Mine, a Superfund site TDC is helping to mitigate—that is, clean up."

"Do they do a lot of that kind of work?" Jason asked. "I thought they were primarily a construction concern."

"They've done some. This is a bigger project, but something they hope to do more of. The federal government is in charge of cleaning up a lot of these old mine sites around the country, but they're spread pretty thin and money is always tight. So someone at TDC approached them with the offer that TDC would do the cleanup in exchange for some other land the government owns, where TDC would like to build a new project. There aren't many companies that could manage something like that, but TDC persuaded the right people that they could."

"Are both these partial reports related to that project?" Jason asked. "And are we supposed to pay attention to the project or just the word *bloody*?"

"I think it's the project. I might be wrong, but this feels right. Dane devoted a lot of hours to this site, and a couple of times he mentioned how complicated and frustrating it was."

Jason watched over her shoulder as she scrolled through the original report on the property—the one that matched the fragment they had received on the first flash drive. "If all of that nasty stuff is in the water," he said, "how do you get it out?"

"There are different ways. You can divert the most poisonous stuff to holding ponds, then use a series of filters to remove the poisons before returning the clean water to the stream. That isn't always practical, so another way is to use settling ponds—divert the water, let it sit for sometimes years, the heavy metals and poisons settling out into gravel. Then that gravel has to be hauled away and disposed of. It's complicated and the process can take years. One of the things Dane did was regularly test the water to see if the levels of harmful substances were dropping."

She pulled up another document. "This is from the files I copied from Dane's computer," she said. "It was created a couple of months ago. See how much the toxin levels have dropped compared to his initial report?"

"That's what they're supposed to do, right?" he asked. "If the site is being decontaminated."

She frowned at the screen, then shook her head. "I'm getting a bad feeling about this."

"What's wrong?" Jason leaned in closer and caught the scent of her hair, subtle and floral. Feminine.

"This was only three months after TDC took over the mitigation at the Mary Lee Mine," she said. "Yet the values on some of these toxins have dropped more than half."

"They were doing a really good job."

She shook her head. "I remember Dane told me it could take a decade or more to clean up some of these sites. Even if you go in and remove all the soil in the waterway, you have to find the source of the contamination and get rid of it, too.

"In the case of mining, that could be tons of waste rock, and materials stored deep in the mine tunnels. One reason these sites take so long to clean up is that there are so many potential sources of contamination, and the materials you're dealing with are so toxic." She glanced at him. "You can't just take what you remove from the area and spread it around somewhere else. It has to be cleaned up before it can go anywhere and, again, that can take years."

"So how did TDC get such an improvement in such a short time?" he asked.

"I don't know. I'm sure Dane was wondering about that, too."

"What about the second flash drive?" Jason asked. "The one that was wrapped in the bandana in the back of Dane's truck?"

"It's another report," she said. "But not a water report. That one deals with contaminants in soil. I haven't found a link to anything on Dane's computer yet."

He put a hand on her shoulder, meaning to reassure her, maybe offer some comfort. "It's been a long day. Time to get some rest." She closed her eyes and rested her cheek against the back of his hand and he froze, fighting a fierce longing to wrap his arms around her and pull her close, to somehow ease some of the burden she carried.

The moment passed. She opened her eyes and sat straight. "I want to go to the Mary Lee Mine," she said.

"Where is it?" Jason asked.

"In the mountains near here. I want to see for myself what TDC is doing up there."

"I'll go with you," he said.

"I didn't invite you."

"I'm inviting myself. I want to see this place, too."

She looked him in the eye and he didn't look away. He was prepared to argue with her about this. If something was going on at that mine that Trask wanted them to know about, no way was he going to let her walk into possible danger alone.

Her smile surprised him, its warmth doing something to his core, making it hard to catch his breath for a few seconds. "All right," she said. "We can go tomorrow, after work. You might be useful to have around, after all."

Useful. Like a tool or a helper. Maybe she did think of him that way. The knowledge rankled, but he was nothing if not stubborn.

And he had always liked a challenge.

By SIX THIRTY on Tuesday morning, Cara had drunk entirely
too much coffee, slept a few fitful hours in her bed while
Jason dozed on the sofa, and learned that Jason Beck was
funny, smart and distractingly sexy in a way that almost
made her forget he was a cop. Warmth spread through
her as she remembered that moment when she had leaned
against him, his hand so comforting and steady on her
shoulder. She wanted to attribute her feelings for him to a
combination of lack of sleep and frayed nerves. But maybe
those weren't the only reasons she felt so unsteady and almost happy around him—though happiness seemed an
impossible emotion, given the seriousness of the situation.
But emotions were fickle, she knew that.

And emotions wouldn't help her find Dane or solve
the puzzle of what he was up to.

She showered, dressed and stumbled into the kitchen
to find Jason scrambling eggs and burning toast. "I
should have warned you, the bread sticks," she said,
yanking the toaster plug from the wall and fishing out
two slices of only slightly too dark bread. "But you
didn't have to fix me breakfast."

"I needed to eat, so I figured you did, too."

Part of the night on her less-than-comfortable sofa
hadn't lessened the man's appeal. The beard stubble
and rumpled shirt gave him a rough-around-the-edges
masculinity that made most of her tingle. Was this what
being in danger did to her—got her all worked up over
the cop who'd come to her rescue?

Jason set a plate of eggs and toast and a mug of coffee
on the table in front of her. "I can follow you to work,
then go home and clean up before my shift," he said.

The scene was so domestic and comforting, as if they were longtime lovers and he spent the night at her place all the time.

Except the closest they had come to intimacy was that almost kiss in this very kitchen before the local police showed up. And surely that had only happened because she was so shaken and dazed by finding out someone had tried to break into her home. She shivered and forced down a swallow of coffee. "I'll call the alarm company as soon as I get to work," she said. She glanced across the table, to where he was shoveling in eggs. Obviously, bad guys didn't lessen his appetite. All in a day's work.

They parted in her driveway and she tried to push down a feeling of dread as she drove to her office.

The engineering department buzzed with conversation when Cara entered, but everyone quieted as she made her way to her desk. She ignored the stares, trying to act as if this was just another day. The thought was comforting—she would get to work at her desk as usual, and any moment now Dane would walk in and she'd find out this had all been a misunderstanding.

She started to stow her purse in the bottom drawer of the desk, but froze as she caught sight of a black-bordered notice someone had laid over her computer keyboard, where she would be sure to see it.

Memorial Service for Dane Trask
Saturday, April 25
10:00 a.m. Canyon Ballroom

"That was posted on the bulletin board in our break room this morning." Maisie came to stand beside Cara, a worried expression on her elfin features.

"How can they have a memorial service for Dane?" Cara asked. "He isn't dead." Jason would have told her if Dane's body had been found—wouldn't he?

She reread the notice twice, but it still didn't make sense.

"So you didn't already know about this?" Maisie asked.

Cara shook her head. "No." She picked up the notice, folded it in two, and slid it into her purse.

"Where are you going?" Maisie asked as Cara turned to leave.

"I'm going to find out more about this," she said.

She paused outside the elevator, studying the company directory and considering her options. When the elevator car arrived, she stepped inside and pressed 7. Executive offices. She might as well go all the way to the top.

Mitchell Ruffino occupied a large suite of offices in the corner of the top floor, with a breathtaking view of Black Canyon and the snowcapped peaks of the San Juan range. But before Cara could reach him, she had to get past his administrative assistant—a very attractive blonde with a close-fitting suit and an icy expression. "You can't see Mr. Ruffino without an appointment," she said, her gaze sliding over—and past—Cara.

"I need to speak with him about this memorial service for Dane Trask." Cara unfolded the notice and showed it to the woman. "I'm Mr. Trask's admin."

The woman scanned the notice. "What about it?"

"I need to speak with Mr. Ruffino." She met the blonde's icy stare with an even chillier one of her own. After what seemed like five minutes but was probably only a few seconds, the blonde picked up her phone. "Have a seat over there," she said.

Heart pounding, Cara perched on the edge of a stylish though uncomfortable chair. Maybe she should leave and go back to her desk before she made things worse for herself and Dane. If TDC wanted to have a memorial service for someone who wasn't dead, why did she care? When Dane was found, he'd probably laugh about it.

A slightly older, dark-haired woman approached Cara. "Mr. Ruffino can give you five minutes," she said. Without waiting for an answer, she turned and walked away.

Cara hurried after her. The woman stopped before a set of double doors. "Go in," she said.

Cara took a deep breath then shoved on the door. Mitchell Ruffino sat behind a desk the size of a pool table, in an office that was easily as large as one floor of Cara's home. "Shara said you wanted to speak with me about Dane Trask's memorial service," he said.

She walked to the desk and stood, back straight and head up, determined not to look like a schoolkid called to the principal's office. She was prepared to look Ruffino in the eye, except that he never lifted his gaze to meet hers. "Dane isn't dead," she said. "How can you hold a memorial for him?"

"This isn't the same as a funeral," Ruffino said with the patient air of someone explaining a simple concept to a dim child. "This is merely a memorial to commemorate what Dane Trask meant to this company."

"But you're accusing him of stealing from you," Cara said. "Why would you even want to memorialize his time with the company?"

"I'm sure the theft was merely the result of an undiagnosed mental illness, perhaps the result of his time in the war," Ruffino said. "We can acknowledge that, and acknowledge the many contributions Dane made to this company. We want to show the public that we're not the villains here."

Nausea churned her stomach. "So this is just some kind of twisted publicity stunt?"

"The public is always watching what we do," Ruffino said. "If more companies remembered that, maybe they would strive to do more good."

She stared at him. What kind of non-answer was that? Apparently, it was the only answer she was going to get. Ruffino picked up his phone and gave her a pointed look. "You should get back to work now."

Back at her desk, Cara stared at her phone for a long moment before she picked it up and punched in Jason's number. He answered on the second ring. "Cara? Is everything all right?"

"TDC just announced that they're holding a memorial service for Dane on Saturday morning."

"A memorial service? But Dane hasn't been declared dead."

"That's what I said, but it turns out this is someone's idea of a good way to make TDC look all forgiving and understanding and righteous—or something.

Dane may have stolen from them, but they're willing to honor him anyway."

"That doesn't really make sense," Jason said.

"Will you come to the service?"

"Oh yeah. I want to get a closer look at the TDC executives, if nothing else," he said. "And I think we need to wait to visit the mine."

"Why?"

"For one thing, I'd like to gather a little more background on the place. For another, we might learn something useful at this service Saturday."

"I doubt that," she said. "I think it's all for show."

"Humor me. We can check out the mine on Sunday."

"All right, it's a date."

He chuckled, and embarrassment flooded her. Why had she said that? She and Jason were not dating. They were involved in a serious investigation. "I'll see you Saturday," he said and ended the call. But he couldn't stop her from fretting over whether she was upset over Dane or over the fact that a cop had her in such turmoil.

Chapter Ten

Dane's memorial was held in a large meeting space TDC used for business seminars and public events. Cara, dressed in a black dress and low heels, had to push past a line of reporters and cameramen to reach the entrance, but they all ignored her. They were probably waiting around for a statement from Mr. Ruffino.

"Cara, over here!"

Cara whipped her head around and found Audra waving from a back corner of the room. Relieved to spot someone who shared her dismay and grief, Cara hurried toward Dane's daughter. Audra wore a bright red dress, a red scarf wound in her long hair. "Red was—is—Dad's favorite color," she said when she caught Cara staring at the dress.

"Your father loves you in anything," Cara said.

"You know Eve Shea, right?" Audra turned to introduce the slim blonde to her left. Dane's former girlfriend looked pale and weary, but she mustered a weak smile.

"Of course Cara and I know each other," Eve said. She glanced around them. "Do you have any idea what is behind this farce? How can you have a memorial service when you don't have a body or even confirmation of a death?"

"I don't know," Cara said. That was easier, and probably less upsetting, than trying to explain the publicity stunt angle.

"It's almost time to start." Audra took Cara's arm. "We need to take our seats up front."

Eve took a step back. "Those seats are for family," she said. "I don't think—"

"I'm not going to sit up there by myself," Audra said. She took hold of Eve's arm with her free hand. "You two can pretend you're my aunts or cousins or something, if it makes you feel better."

"All right," Eve said as Audra marched them toward the front of the room. "But I'm not sure Dane would want me here. I'm the one who broke things off between us, after all."

"I want you here," Audra said.

They were almost to their seats when Bert Levy, from the surveying department, stepped into the aisle. "I'm sorry you have to go through this, Audra," Bert said, his watery brown eyes downcast. He ran a big hand through his thinning blond hair. "They're not really saying Dane is dead, are they?"

"Until they show me a body, I won't believe my father is dead," Audra said. She flicked the ends of her scarf over her shoulder. "This is just a show TDC is putting on to mollify their conscience."

The lines on either side of Bert's mouth deepened. "Some of us wanted to put together teams to search for Dane," he said. "But when I took the idea to Mr. Ruffino, he shut me right down. He said it was too dangerous and we needed to leave it to the professionals."

"Well, thank you for trying, Bert." Audra patted his hand. "Thank you a lot."

The three women had just settled into their seats on the first row, just below the raised dais, on which was centered a large photograph of Dane, when a commotion behind them made them turn to look.

Jason Beck and Officer Hudson stood in the middle of the aisle. Each of them wore simple, dark suits with white shirts and understated ties. But the civilian clothes did nothing to hide the fact that they were law enforcement. Their erect posture and the wary way they continually scanned the crowd gave away their profession.

Jason's eyes met and held Cara's gaze. Something stirred in her, an emotion she didn't want to examine too closely. "Why is he always looking at me like that?" Audra whispered.

Cara blinked. Jason had been looking at her, not Audra. She started to say as much when she realized Audra was referring to Jason's partner. Officer Hudson had his eyes fixed on Dane's daughter.

"I wouldn't call that a bad look," Eve said. "I'd say the hunky cop is interested in you. And not as a suspect in any crime."

"Oh really," Audra said. Her cheeks flushed a deeper pink and she fluffed her hair before she turned to face forward once more.

Jason and Hud slid into chairs two rows behind and across the aisle from Cara and the other two women. She forced herself to face the dais as the lights dimmed and Mitchell Ruffino strode to the podium. "Thank you for coming today to honor a man who contributed a great deal to the success of TDC Enterprises in the past six years," he said. "At TDC we believe in acknowledging the contributions of our employees, and wanted to do so for Dane Trask, before any more recent events are allowed to tarnish his memory."

"This is the kookiest event I've ever been to," Eve, seated on Cara's right, muttered.

"Hush," Audra said as a screen rose from the center of the stage. Music swelled and a photograph appeared of Dane standing with a group of men in suits, each holding a shovel. Dane, in khakis and boots, the sleeves of his white dress shirt rolled up to reveal tanned forearms, stood out from the crowd of executives. Here was clearly a man who didn't spend all his time seated behind a desk.

The slide shifted to one of Dane making a presentation at a conference. Then the slides shifted abruptly to photos of a younger Dane in uniform. A murmur rose from the crowd, and Ruffino began to read a list of Dane's military accomplishments—battles he was part of, medals and commendations he had received.

"Dane Trask made a great sacrifice to serve his country," Ruffino intoned. "But as we all know, the effects of war do not end upon discharge from service. Dane Trask was not immune to the mental wounds battle can inflict."

"Dane would have hated this," Eve fumed. "This whole assumption that every soldier must have something wrong with him. That, of course, they're all too messed up to function in society. He worked hard to dispel those stereotypes."

"Dad was saner than any of us," Audra agreed. She sniffed and blotted tears.

Cara squeezed Audra's arm. Inside, she was seething. She thought she knew what Ruffino was doing here. When Dane was found, the press and public would discredit anything he said because, after all, he was struggling with mental problems brought on by his war service. She didn't believe that for one second. Whatever had been bothering Dane over the last few weeks, she was pretty sure it had nothing to do with the war.

The last photograph was a blow-up of Dane's company identification picture. He stared into the camera with a serious expression, a handsome man in his prime, who managed to appear smart and capable in what was essentially a corporate mug shot.

Ruffino droned on about Dane's accomplishments for TDC. "You will be hearing other things from TDC in the coming days about Dane Trask, some of it not very pleasant. But now is not the time for those. Today, we are remembering the good things Dane did, and the good man he was."

Audra bowed her head and began to sob. Cara slipped her arm around Audra's shoulders and glared toward the podium. The longer she sat there, the more furious she became.

Ruffino—who had been the only person to speak—concluded his remarks and dismissed the gathering. He had scarcely moved away from the podium when Jason was at her side. "I think Ruffino should be glad looks can't really kill," he said. "The way you were staring at him sure looked lethal."

"He's lying about Dane having any kind of mental or emotional problems related to the war or anything else," she said. "Dane was all for getting help for people who needed it, but he despised the way too many people saw every soldier as troubled or messed up." She looked around at the crowd of press and coworkers, along with some Welcome Home Warriors members who had come to honor Dane. "This whole event was just a twisted way for TDC to pat themselves on the back before they get on with destroying Dane's reputation."

"Let's go outside where we can talk," Jason said. He took her hand and led her out a side door, into a walled courtyard furnished with benches and a burbling fountain. The gurgle of the water helped to drown out the murmur of the crowd leaving the auditorium.

Cara turned to face him. "Bert Levy, one of the TDC surveyors, told me he and some others wanted to organize teams to look for Dane, and Ruffino told him to leave that work to the professionals."

"Ruffino gave him good advice," Jason said. "The last thing we want is someone else lost or injured in that rugged country." He patted her shoulder. "Sometimes things that seem suspicious are just big companies protecting themselves—from true liability, or many just from bad press. That's probably what was behind this show today."

"Don't patronize me!" she snapped.

He took a step back. "I would never do that."

The intensity of his gaze, and the edge of anger in

his voice, made her flinch. But she couldn't look away. Maybe he wasn't patronizing her. Maybe it was only her own helplessness making her feel this way. "Doesn't it bother you?" she asked. "Trying to find answers, yet only coming up against more questions?"

"It can be frustrating," he said. "But it's part of the job. People lie, and they try to hide things. You have to admit, if Dane wants us to know something, it would be a lot easier if he'd come out and tell us, instead of leaving cryptic hints."

"Maybe he can't come out and tell us," she said. "Maybe someone is watching him. Guarding him. He has to be careful."

"Who's guarding him? Who's watching him?"

She squeezed the sides of her head. "More questions I don't have the answers to."

"Try to trust that I'm looking for the answers to those same questions," he said.

"Don't shut me out of the investigation," she said. "Let me help you. And where I can't help, don't leave me in the dark about what's going on." She moved closer and touched the back of his hand. "I don't want to interfere or to tell you how to do your job. I just want to know that you're still trying to help. Don't give up on Dane."

He took her hand and squeezed it. "I'll tell you as much as I can." When she started to protest, he continued. "If I don't tell you something, it's because legally I can't, or because doing so might compromise our case, or even put you in danger. But I won't leave you to wonder and worry. I won't give up on Dane, and

I won't give up on you." He released her hand. "Maybe we'll find out more when we visit the Mary Lee Mine tomorrow. If you still want to go?"

"Of course I want to go," she said.

"Great. I'll pick you up about ten."

"Cara, we're over here!" Audra's shout and wave distracted her, and when she looked back again, Jason was gone. But his last words echoed in her mind. He wanted her to trust him, and she had never needed to trust someone more.

SUNDAY MORNING, JASON arrived at Cara's house promptly at 10:00 a.m., driving his Ranger Brigade SUV and in full uniform. "You look very official," she said as she slid into the passenger seat.

"Yeah, well, sometimes the uniform opens doors and inspires cooperation." He looked rueful. "And sometimes it doesn't."

They drove for forty-five minutes, making small talk about nothing important. Cara wondered if he was purposefully avoiding mentioning the case or what they might find at the mine. Or maybe he was just someone who didn't have a lot to say in the morning.

The Forest Service road that led to the Mary Lee Mine had recently been widened and covered with a thick layer of gravel. The stumps of trees cut to effect this transformation stuck up like broken teeth along the roadside. After two miles of them listening to the gravel ping off the underside of the SUV, the road stopped at an iron gate, eight feet tall and twelve feet wide, equipped with a keypad, a speaker and the single glaring eye of a camera.

Jason pulled up to the speaker and keypad and lowered his window. He pressed the button on the speaker and waited. Nothing happened. He pushed the button again. "Hello?" Again, there was no response.

"Care to guess the gate code?" Jason asked. "Maybe something you use at TDC?"

Cara shook her head. "We don't have a gate at TDC."

He studied the area for a long moment, then turned the SUV around and drove back down the road a quarter mile, pulled off to the side and cut the engine. "What now?" she asked.

"I thought we'd take a little hike."

Cara looked down at her shoes. They were flats, not heels, but not designed for rugged country. "I don't know how far I'll get in these shoes."

Jason opened the driver's-side door. "You're welcome to wait for me here. It would probably be safer if you did."

"You're not leaving me behind." She slid to the ground and came around to meet him.

He handed her a bottle of water from a cooler in the rear of the SUV and grinned. "I never thought you would, but it's fun to get a rise out of you."

It wasn't "you're beautiful when you're angry," but it was close enough. She debated pouring the water on him, but she was thirsty, so she settled for glaring at him. He laughed and she felt the sound somewhere below her navel. That was the confusing thing about all her dealings with Jason Beck. Her lips said one thing but her body was having an entirely different conversation.

JASON AND CARA hiked away from the SUV, through the woods roughly parallel to the gate and the tall fence on either side of it. Jason waited for Cara to ask where they were going, but she remained silent, except for the occasional curse when she stumbled on the rough ground. He would have insisted she stay behind if he had had any hope of her agreeing. As it was, he felt better having her with him. He could keep her safe—from what or who, he couldn't say—and she was more likely to recognize something out of place at the mine.

When they had been walking about ten minutes, he stopped and waited for her to catch up. "What are we looking for up here?" he asked. "At the mine site?"

"I don't know," she said. "I only visited a reclamation site once, and that was before I worked for TDC. It was just a couple of big hills with grass growing on them. A sign explained that the hills topped clay bunkers full of hazardous waste dug from the ground around the mine, and the holding ponds behind the hills were collecting more hazardous sediment that filtered out from the water. Once clean, the water was diverted back to its original channel."

"So we're looking for digging or earth-moving equipment? Things like that?"

"I think so." She looked toward where they could glimpse chain-link fencing through the trees. "But we're not going to see anything if we can't get past that fence."

"Let's keep walking," he said. "Maybe we'll find a

way." It didn't seem practical to him to fence off the entire property, which was just under five acres. Especially with no near neighbors, no close-by hiking trails, and the only road being the one that led to the locked gate.

Ten minutes later, the fence abruptly ended. No other fence bisected it and no cameras surveilled the area, unless they were hidden. A single red-and-white sign proclaimed Danger! Entry Forbidden!

He took Cara's hand and led her around the fence, past the sign. They were now officially trespassing. Not the best position for a law enforcement officer to be in. His goal was to get in and get out as quickly as possible. If he spotted anything suspicious, he'd do his best to obtain a legal warrant to check things out.

He guided them back toward the gate, reasoning that any heavy equipment in use on the property had entered from that direction. They wound around thick knots of pinion, through the slender white trunks of aspen and over outcroppings of rough granite, until they stood at the edge of a clearing, mounds of rocks like crumbling pyramids all around them.

They picked their way around the rocks, piles of various-size stones in half a dozen shades of gray. Cara stooped and picked up a small chunk and slipped it into her pocket. Jason pretended not to notice. "Did all of this come out of the mine?" he asked.

"I don't know," she said. "I think at least some of this is mine waste—the stuff left over after the ore is removed. That's what makes those big yellow-and-orange spills you see down the sides of mountains. A lot of the mines themselves are flooded. When they were working mines, pumps ran all the time to keep out the water. Now the water fills up the tunnels and leaches harmful chemicals out of the rock."

"And the radioactive stuff?" he asked. "Where does that come from?"

"That comes from rock," she said. "Uranium ore. But I'm not sure if they mine that in this area. I thought that was farther south and west of here."

"Dane's report mentioned a couple of radioactive isotopes."

"That's true. Maybe they did mine uranium here. I'll have to do more research."

He put a hand on her arm. "Let's get a little closer to the gate and see what we can see."

The area around the gate looked deserted, save for a small, locked shed. Cara turned in a full circle, surveying the area. "I really don't see anything that looks suspicious," she said.

Then the first gunshot exploded in the rocks to her left.

Chapter Eleven

Cara heard the loud report and looked up to see Jason launch himself at her. They hit the ground together, hard, as more bullets thudded into the dirt around them.

Someone was shooting at them? Why?

Jason rolled with her to the cover of a depression in the trees then rose up on one elbow, weapon in his other hand. "Stay down!" he barked.

"I think I'm smart enough to figure that out on my own," she muttered as she pressed herself as far into the dirt as possible. Her heart beat painfully. Was it possible to die of fear before a bullet found her?

The reports sounded even louder now, then she realized Jason was returning fire. She pressed her hands tightly to her ears, closed her eyes and mashed her cheek into the dirt.

She didn't know how long she lay there before she felt a gentle tug on her arm. She opened her eyes, prepared to lash out at anyone who tried to drag her away, and met Jason's concerned gaze. "I think they're gone," he said. "We need to get out of here."

He helped her to her feet. "Are you okay?" he asked.

She nodded. "Are you?"

"Yeah. Come on." He paused at the edge of their cover to collect several of the spent bullets and drop them into his pocket. Then they retreated the way they had come, jogging over the rough ground, arriving at the SUV, panting hard.

She slid into the passenger seat and buckled the seat belt with shaking hands as he started the engine. "That's a pretty extreme reaction to trespassers," she said when her breathing had slowed to almost normal.

"I don't think they were serious about killing us," he said.

"Those bullets seemed pretty serious to me."

"They had us cornered," he said. "They could have moved in and finished us off. Instead, they left. I think they just wanted to frighten us."

"They succeeded." She pressed a hand to her chest, as if that could calm her still wildly beating heart. "Did you ever see anyone? All I got a good look at was the ground underneath those trees."

"No. They were firing from behind the shed, I think."

"I never saw another vehicle," she said.

"I didn't, either. But it could have been parked out of sight somewhere nearby."

"Are you going to report this?" she asked.

He glanced at her. "I probably should."

"But you'd have to admit you were trespassing. And that you didn't find anything."

"I would."

"Or you could say you were there at the request of a TDC employee," she said.

"Are you authorized to visit TDC work sites?"

"No, but it would take some digging to find that out. I work for the company and I don't even know where you'd get that information. And it's not a lie. I work for TDC. I asked you to come with me."

"I insisted on going with you."

"If I hadn't wanted you along, I could have figured out how to give you the slip."

"You sound pretty sure of yourself."

"I can be devious when I have to be."

He must have heard the laughter behind her words because the dimple on the right side of his mouth deepened with his smile. When was the last time she had flirted with a man like this—and enjoyed it so much?

"Want to go somewhere and grab a bite to eat?" he asked. "I don't feel like going home just yet."

Was he asking her out? On a date?

No. A date required planning. Washing her hair and shaving her legs. This was just two people who happened to be together at dinnertime. "All right. Anything but sushi."

He shook his head. "And here I was going to suggest sushi." When he winked, she couldn't help but laugh, even as a sinking feeling settled in the pit of her stomach. If she didn't watch herself, she'd fall fast for Jason. And everybody knew speeding was bound to get you in trouble.

JASON ASKED CARA to choose a restaurant and she suggested an Italian bistro housed in a former Victorian home. Diners sat at white-clothed tables, two to three per room, classical music playing softly on hidden speakers. It was a lot more romantic than he had anticipated, but the diners were casually dressed and the prices modest, so he began to relax a little and enjoy the calming atmosphere and the pleasant company.

Cara had persuaded him to stop by her house so that she could wash the streaks of dirt from her face and hands and change into jeans and a flowing blouse that brought out the green of her eyes. She'd put on pink lipstick and dusted on some face powder, hiding the freckles he found so appealing. He'd taken the opportunity to clean up, also, and to change into the jeans and button-down shirt he kept in a bag in the back of the SUV.

"Tell me how you ended up in Montrose," he said after they had given their order for dinner.

"I came for the job," she said. "I was living in Texas at the time and wanted to move to Colorado. I started looking for work, applied online, and was hired after a phone interview. I'd never even heard of Montrose before, but after I got here, I fell in love with this area— the river, the canyons, the mountains. There's a little of everything here. What about you?"

"I came for work, too."

"Right. So where's your family?"

"My mom and dad are in New Hampshire. I have one sister in Upstate New York. What about your family?"

"My parents are in Houston. My brother was my only sibling." She looked away, her expression more guarded. "After Corey died, my parents sort of fell apart. He was their baby and, I guess, kind of the glue that held us all together."

"I imagine a loss like that is hard to get past."

"It is. But I don't want to talk about Corey tonight. Or about Dane."

"What do you want to talk about?"

"Books, movies. The kinds of things people talk about when they're getting to know each other."

She didn't say "when they're on a first date" but that's what this felt like. So, over homemade pasta and a bottle of red wine, they discussed books—she admitted to being a fan of suspense novels—sports—she loved baseball and hated football—and music—singer-song-writers and older rock and roll were at the top of her list.

By the time they had finished the last of the bottle of wine and eaten the last piece of bread, the candle at their table had guttered out and the street outside the restaurant was dark.

As they walked to his SUV, he slipped an arm around her waist and she didn't object. He didn't want the evening to end. Should he suggest going somewhere for coffee?

She stopped suddenly, so that he stumbled on the uneven sidewalk. Before he could speak, she gripped his hand, hard. "That car parked at the curb across the street…" she said. "Look, but don't let the driver see you looking."

He knelt and pretended to tie the laces of his hiking boot, and looked past Cara's legs to the dark sedan parked in front of a house that was being remodeled, the front yard filled with a Dumpster and heavy equipment. He made note of what he could see then rose, took Cara's arm and led her along. "Do you recognize him?" he asked.

"I think it's one of the two men who came to Dane's office to collect all his things," she said. "The big black guy."

"Durrell." Jason remembered the name. "I think you're right. Maybe he lives around here."

"Then what is he doing parked across from the restaurant where we just happen to be eating?"

"Maybe he's waiting for someone."

"Or maybe he's watching me."

They reached the SUV and he unlocked it and opened the passenger door for her.

As she swung into the seat, she looked back over her shoulder at him. "You think I'm being paranoid," she said.

"No. I think it's a theory worth testing out."

"How are we going to do that?" she asked.

"Let's see if he follows us."

He drove, not in the direction of Cara's house, but away, toward the reservoir and open road and barren landscape that offered few hiding places. As they left town, he checked his rearview mirror. "I think that's the same car back there," he said.

Cara studied the side mirror. "I think you're right."

Jason slowed but the car behind him slowed, as well, not drawing any closer.

"What do we do now?" Cara asked.

"Maybe we have some fun with him." He gave the

SUV gas, shooting forward until they were doing almost ninety miles an hour.

Cara, white-faced, clutched the armrest. "Do you know what you're doing?" she asked.

"Of course. I'm a trained professional." He slowed abruptly as they crested a hill. The sedan roared up behind him, giving him a clear view of the driver.

"I'm sure that's the man from the restaurant," Cara said.

"The car doesn't have a front plate," Jason said. "But I think it's the same person, too."

The driver dropped back out of sight. "Did he leave?" Cara asked.

"I doubt it," Jason said. He turned left onto a side road, drove to a clump of dense trees on the shoulder and parked beneath them, facing the highway. About a minute later, the sedan passed them.

"Why is he following us?" Cara asked, agitation straining her voice.

"My guess is he thinks you'll lead him to Dane Trask." He put the SUV into gear and pulled onto the highway once more.

Cara turned to watch out the back window. "I think you lost him," she said after a few minutes. She swiveled around and settled into the seat.

"Where do you want to go?" Jason asked.

"Take me home," she said.

He tightened his grip on the steering wheel. "I don't want to frighten you," he said. "But it's possible that's who was trying to break into your place Monday night."

She didn't make a sound but he felt the change in her,

like a drop in the temperature. "I have new locks and an alarm system," she said. "I won't let these people drive me out of my home."

"You're welcome to stay with me tonight. Or I can stay at your place." He tried to make the invitation sound casual. "No strings attached."

"Thank you." She touched his arm, the gentlest brush of her fingers that nevertheless had every nerve standing at attention. "But I think I'll be okay. If he only wants to find out where Dane is, he's wasting his time with me."

What if that's not all he wants? Jason thought but didn't say. "If you see any sign of him or his vehicle, or you see or hear anything suspicious, call 9-1-1," he said. "Then call me."

"I will. I promise."

He drove past her house before stopping, scanning the neighboring driveways for any sign of the dark sedan with no front plate. Cara said nothing. When he came around a second time, he pulled to the curb in front of her house. "Thank you for a lovely evening," she said. "Even if the rest of the day was a little more eventful than I would have liked."

"Thank you for the good company," he said. "If I have to be shot at or tailed, I'd rather do it with you than with anyone else."

She laughed, though he thought it sounded a little forced. "We'll talk more tomorrow," she said.

"Let me walk you to the door."

He took her arm as they proceeded up the walk then took her key, opened the door and walked through the house, checking that everything was in order. She didn't protest, but she didn't invite him to stay, either.

Back at the door, she turned to him. "I'll be okay," she said. "Really."

She looked a lot calmer than he felt. "If you need anything…" he began.

"I'll call you." She pressed a finger to his lips then kissed him gently, a closed-mouth peck that nevertheless had him breaking out in a sweat.

Cara closed the front door behind him and he waited to hear the locks snick into place. He then walked to the SUV, drove around the block and sat parked under a tree. He'd wait here awhile, keeping watch. Just in case.

THE NEXT MORNING, a bleary-eyed Jason, having stayed parked near Cara's house until almost four in the morning, stepped into the office of commander Grant Sanderlin. FBI Special Agent Sanderlin had joined the Ranger Brigade exactly two months prior to Jason's arrival, but had settled into the leadership role quickly. Tall, slender, his sandy-brown hair shot through with silver, he had icy blue eyes, the clipped speech of a New Englander, and a reputation as a strict but fair supervisor.

"I agreed to accompany Cara Mead to the Mary Lee Mine yesterday afternoon," Jason said. "She was uncomfortable going there on her own, given the circumstances surrounding her boss, Dane Trask's, disappearance."

"What circumstances made her fear for her safety?" the commander asked. "Is she fearful Trask might try to harm her? Does she believe he's hiding at the mine?"

"No, sir." Jason had to tread carefully here. He had to justify his actions with facts not supposition. "The flash drive left on the front seat of Ms. Mead's car the day we discovered Trask's truck in the canyon contains a fragment of a water quality report Ms. Mead believes is from the Mary Lee Mine," he said. "TDC has a federal contract to remediate contaminants at the mine site. The fragment of the report on the flash drive is similar to, but different from, the most recent water quality results for that mine, as reported by Trask. A copy of that report was on his work computer, and Ms. Mead reviewed it before she handed all of Trask's files over to us. She wanted to visit the mine to see if she could find anything to account for the differences between the reports."

"What did she expect to find?" Sanderlin asked.

"I'm not sure," Jason said. "In any case, we weren't there long before someone fired on us. A semiautomatic rifle, I think." He laid the spent bullets he had collected from the ground around their hiding place on the desk. "I believe the shooter was deliberately aiming wide," he said. "Not intending to kill us, but to scare us off."

"One shooter?" Sanderlin asked.

"I believe so. I never saw anyone, or any other vehicle, in the area."

Sanderlin studied the bullets. "What does Ms. Mead say? Does TDC have an overzealous security guard? Or a trigger-happy squatter?"

"She hasn't found out anything yet," Jason said. If she had, she would have called him.

"Sit down." Sanderlin gestured to the chair across

from his desk. Jason sat and the commander regarded him with a measuring gaze. "Last night I saw the news report about Dane Trask," he said. "The coverage portrayed him as a troubled veteran with financial difficulties."

"My investigation so far hasn't borne that out," Jason said. "Dane Trask is a former Army Ranger who served in Afghanistan and Iraq. Since his discharge, he founded an organization—Welcome Home Warriors—that provides services for veterans. The organization, and Trask himself, have a good reputation."

"What does Ms. Mead say about her boss?"

"She believes he's innocent of any wrongdoing and may be in trouble," Jason said.

"Were she and Mr. Trask romantically involved?"

Jason was beginning to understand Cara's annoyance with everyone asking that question. "No, sir," he said. "They had a professional relationship only."

"Emotions can color how the individual interprets facts," Sanderlin said. "That's why it's worth knowing about any connections between the principals."

"Yes, sir."

"TDC seems very certain about their assessment of the situation," Sanderlin said. "If Trask is still alive and operating in our territory, we need to respect that he may be exactly what TDC says he is—desperate and potentially dangerous."

"Yes, sir." Even if Cara was right about Dane's innocence, the man's military background made him capable of violence, especially if he felt cornered. "I'm

Get Up To 4 Free Books!

Dear Reader,

IT'S A FACT: if you answer 4 quick questions, we'll send you 4 FREE REWARDS from each series you try!

Try **Harlequin® Romantic Suspense** books featuring heart-racing page-turners with unexpected plot twists and irresistible chemistry that will keep you guessing to the very end.

Try **Harlequin Intrigue® Larger-Print** books featuring action-packed stories that will keep you on the edge of your seat. Solve the crime and deliver justice at all costs.

Or **TRY BOTH!**

I'm not kidding you. As a leading publisher of women's fiction, we value your opinions... and your time. That's why we are prepared to reward you handsomely for completing our mini-survey. In fact, we have 4 Free Rewards for you, including 2 free books and 2 free gifts from each series you try!

Thank you for participating in our survey,

Pam Powers

To get your 4 FREE REWARDS:
Complete the survey below and return the insert today to receive up to 4 FREE BOOKS and FREE GIFTS guaranteed!

"4 for 4" MINI-SURVEY

1 Is reading one of your favorite hobbies?
☐ YES ☐ NO

2 Do you prefer to read instead of watch TV?
☐ YES ☐ NO

3 Do you read newspapers and magazines?
☐ YES ☐ NO

4 Do you enjoy trying new book series with FREE BOOKS?
☐ YES ☐ NO

Please send me my Free Rewards, consisting of **2 Free Books from each series I select** and **Free Mystery Gifts.** I understand that I am under no obligation to buy anything, as explained on the back of this card.

☐ **Harlequin® Romantic Suspense** (240/340 HDL GQ5A)
☐ **Harlequin Intrigue® Larger-Print** (199/399 HDL GQ5A)
☐ **Try Both** (240/340 & 199/399 HDL GQ5M)

FIRST NAME	LAST NAME

ADDRESS

APT.#	CITY

STATE/PROV.	ZIP/POSTAL CODE

EMAIL ☐ Please check this box if you would like to receive newsletters and promotional emails from Harlequin Enterprises ULC and its affiliates. You can unsubscribe anytime.

HI/HRS-520-MS20

HARLEQUIN READER SERVICE—Here's how it works:

focused on finding Trask," he said. "Any other criminal charges will be the sheriff's concern."

"It's possible Trask is the person who fired on you yesterday," Sanderlin said. "He may have had another vehicle stashed somewhere, or he may have an accomplice."

"I'm looking into that," Jason said.

"If you find evidence that points to Trask hiding out at the mine, I'll authorize seeking a search warrant," Sanderlin said.

"Thank you, sir. That's not the only suspicious incident yesterday, unfortunately," Jason said.

"What else?"

"When I was driving Ms. Mead home, we noticed a car following us. She recognized the driver as an employee of TDC. He was one of the men assigned to collected Trask's files and computer, before we took them into custody as evidence. I recognized him, also. He followed for quite a while until I evaded him. I stayed parked near Ms. Mead's home for several hours after that, but didn't see him again."

"You're certain he was following you."

"Yes, sir."

Sanderlin considered the new information. "Do you think this was the same person who fired on you and Ms. Mead at the Mary Lee Mine?"

"I don't know."

"I don't think there's any action we can take right now, but keep me updated."

When Jason returned to his desk, Hud was leaning

against it, arms crossed. "How did things go with Ms. Mead yesterday?" he asked.

"Fine." Certainly their dinner had been pleasant, and though her kiss good-night had been brief, he'd felt real emotion behind it.

"I had an interesting call while you were out joy-riding with the lovely Ms. Mead," Hud said.

"Oh? What was it?" Hud had the look of a man with an interesting story to tell.

"The Smokeys have a campground thief that has them stumped."

Jason didn't even wince at the slang for park rangers. He'd heard much worse. "What is it? A clever chipmunk or maybe a bold bear?"

"No, they're pretty sure this one is human," Hud said. "Because it doesn't just take things—it leaves other things in exchange."

Jason leaned forward, suddenly more interested. "What kind of things does he steal?" he asked.

"Food, mostly. A water bottle. Soap. Nothing really valuable, but it freaks people out, you know?"

"And what does this thief leave in exchange?" Jason asked.

"A few times the guy left money, but most of the time it's other stuff. A penlight. A fishing lure. A stick carved into a squirrel." Hud shook his head. "But I was thinking you might be interested."

"Maybe it's Dane Trask," Jason said. "Sneaking into the campground to get things he needs and leaving items in trade."

"That's my guess, too," Hud said. "The park rangers

haven't hit on that suspicion yet, so I didn't mention it, though you can, if you want. For now, they're playing things close to the vest. They don't want to panic the tourists, but they're planning to set a trap for the thief."

"What kind of trap?"

"They're setting up a fake campsite, complete with a cooler full of goodies and a picnic table set for a party. They're going to have two rangers in a blind nearby, ready to pounce." He rapped his knuckles on the desk. "With luck, Trask could be in custody by tomorrow."

Would Cara be cheered by this news or even more distressed at the thought of Dane in jail?

Chapter Twelve

Chaos greeted Cara at TDC headquarters Monday morning. No one was at their desk, and the din of conversation drowned out the piped-in music. "What's going on?" she asked Maisie, who was passing her desk with a large potted palm hugged to her chest.

"The big bosses are here and there's going to be a press conference. Come on, help me with these plants." She shoved the palm into Cara's arms and retrieved a four-foot-tall ficus tree from its normal resting place behind Cara's desk.

Cara followed her friend through the crowd to the elevator, finally emerging on the second floor and making their way to a large conference room.

"Put the palm at that end of the dais," Maisie directed. "Behind the ferns."

Cara did as instructed, while Maisie arranged the ficus at the opposite end of the dais, which had been set up with a skirted conference table and four chairs.

As she was wondering who the chairs were for, VP Mitchell Ruffino entered, followed by Charles Terrell, Gary Davis and Drew Compton.

Maisie grabbed Cara's arm and dragged her out the door on the opposite side of the room. "The last thing you want is for one of them to notice you for the wrong reason," Maisie said.

Cara shook free of her friend's grip. "What is going on?" she asked. "What's the press conference about?"

"I have no idea," Maisie said. "But it must be big, if all three of the bigwigs are here."

A crowd of what was clearly media, complete with shoulder-held cameras, large microphones and on-air makeup, hurried past. "Come on," Maisie said. "We can stand at the back of the room and watch."

Charles Terrell, silver glinting in his brown hair and close-cropped goatee, looked more like a movie star than a CEO. The other partners in the firm, portly, balding Gary Davis and rail-thin, curly haired Drew Compton, looked even homelier next to Terrell, but all three conveyed an air of grave seriousness as they filed onto the dais and took their seats before the press and assorted onlookers.

Mr. Ruffino, in a funeral-worthy black suit, stood at the microphone and scowled like a disapproving priest. "On behalf of TDC Enterprises, I am going to read a statement," he said. "Then we will entertain brief questions."

He studied the paper in his hand for a long moment as flashbulbs flared and cameras hummed. Then he cleared his throat and began to read.

"'It is with great regret that I must inform you that an engineer formerly employed with TDC Enterprises, Dane Trask, is now a fugitive from justice. Mr. Trask, whom we believe has embezzled a large sum from our company, disappeared shortly after the decision was made to file charges against him. He is still at large and is considered armed and dangerous.'"

Cara gasped as a larger-than-life-size image of Dane appeared on a screen behind Ruffino's shoulder. In the photo, he was dressed for a hike and smiling, the dramatic painted cliffs of Black Canyon of Gunnison National Park rising behind him. Ironically, TDC had used the same image at Dane's memorial service on Saturday.

"'If you encounter this individual, do not attempt to confront him yourself,'" Ruffino continued reading. "'We ask that you call the hotline number we have established. TDC is offering a $25,000 reward for information leading to the apprehension of Trask.'"

Ruffino looked up from the paper. More flashbulbs flared and a chorus of voices rose.

"How much money did Dane Trask steal?"

"Why such a large reward?"

"What was Trask's job with TDC?"

"How did you uncover the embezzlement?"

"Where was Trask last seen?"

"Are you saying now the memorial service you held for Trask on Saturday was premature?"

The questions rose from all sides, many repeated more than once. Instead of answering them, Terrell took Ruffino's place at the microphone and spoke about how this unfortunate episode didn't erode his faith in the many loyal employees of TDC. "One bad apple will not spoil the whole crop," he declared. "TDC will continue its commitment to quality work and community involvement in the future."

"So Dane really did steal from the company!" Maisie spoke softly, but there was no missing her excitement. "And now he's on the run. It's like a movie or some-thing."

Cara wanted to protest that Dane hadn't stolen any-thing, and that he wasn't dangerous, but how did she know that for sure?

Ruffino announced that the press conference was over. Terrell, Davis and Compton filed out of the room and a couple of uniformed security guards began usher-ing everyone into the hallway. Cara slipped away from Maisie to the stairs, using the climb to the fifth floor to try to organize her thoughts.

A few days ago, Ruffino had said Dane had stolen a hundred thousand dollars but the company wanted to hold a memorial service and heap praises on him any-way. It was a lot of money, but a huge enterprise like TDC could deduct such a loss from taxes, and maybe the powers-that-be thought singing Dane's praises would score them a lot of good publicity.

What had happened to change their minds? Why offer one-quarter of the amount Dane had supposedly stolen as a reward? Why alert the public when local law enforcement was already searching for Dane?

She slipped into her office and made her way to her desk. Sinking into the chair, she swiveled toward her computer, hoping to distract herself by reading through old files and reports. But the computer wasn't there. She blinked, then noticed other things missing. Her in- and out-boxes were both empty and the desk calendar with a bad pun for each day was gone.

Heart racing, she pulled open the center drawer. A few paperclips and stray pens lingered in space that had previously held her spare change, a pack of gum, bandages, aspirin and a nail file.

The other drawers of the desk were completely empty, except for her purse. Everything else that was hers, or was related to her work, was gone.

CARA LEFT THE office. She didn't say anything to anyone, she simply walked out. After the shock of the press conference, she was in no mood to track down her few belongings from that desk. She could deal with that tomorrow.

She got in the car, intending to drive until she had come to some conclusion about the next step she should take. Jason would probably tell her to trust him and his colleagues to find Dane, but the cops assigned to her brother's case had said much the same and had ended up doing nothing. She hadn't been able to help her brother, but she might be able to help Dane. That thought made it impossible to sit at home and do nothing.

She ended up at Black Canyon of Gunnison National Park, maybe out of some subconscious desire to retrace Dane's steps, to figure out what had gotten into his head that day. As she parked at the Dragon Point overlook, she was startled to find two Ranger Brigade SUVs, and Jason with Officer Hudson.

"Cara, what are you doing here?" Jason asked as she approached.

"Have you found any sign of Dane?" she asked. "I'm worried he might be out there alone and hurt."

"We don't know for sure the blood we found was his," Hud said. "Only his type."

"Blood?" She staggered, suddenly dizzy. "What blood? Dane's blood? Where?"

Jason grabbed her arms, steadying her. "The bandana the second flash drive was wrapped in had some bloodstains. Not a lot of blood." He glared at Hud. "It matches Dane's blood type, but it wasn't necessarily a recent stain. It could have been from a long time ago. And it might have been from someone besides Dane."

She pulled out of his grasp. "Why didn't you tell me?"

"I didn't tell you because I didn't want to upset you."

"I'm already upset. Or hadn't you realized?"

Hud's shoulder-mounted radio crackled and he turned away. Jason looked back to Cara, his arms outstretched, as if he wanted to touch her again. But he kept his distance. "We haven't found any more blood," he said. "It may not even be significant."

"You've spent how many hours at my house the past few days and you didn't think to mention this? I thought you weren't going to shut me out. But that's exactly what you're doing."

"I need to go," Hud said, taking a few steps toward them.

"Do you need help?" Jason asked. Did she imagine the desperation in his eyes?

"No." Hud glanced at Cara. "You'd better stay here and take care of this."

Cara glared at him. She was not a "this."

After Hudson left, Jason moved to her side. "What are you doing here?" he asked. "Why aren't you at work?"

"You're telling me the truth about the blood? There wasn't much of it, and you haven't found any more?"

"Yes. We've been searching for several days and we haven't found anything." He took her arm. "I know you want to stay informed about this case, but it would be irresponsible of me to tell you about something—like that bloodstain—before we knew for sure it even pertained to the case. And though you don't want to hear it, I'm going to say this anyway. You're Dane's friend. You're not another investigator. I can't share everything with you."

She stared at the ground, the truth of his words grating. "Just don't keep anything really important from me, okay?"

He squeezed gently. "Okay. Now, what are you doing here? You're obviously upset."

"TDC held a press conference this morning," she said. "Mitch Ruffino, Charles Terrell, Gary Davis and Drew Compton—TDC—were all there. I've never seen all of them together in one place like that. Terrell lives in Hawaii, I think, and Davis and Compton are in Denver. But this was important enough to get all of them together in one place."

Jason waited, eyes fixed on her, but not pressuring her. She wondered if he was naturally so patient or if it was something he had learned on the job. "They announced that Dane had stolen a lot of money from the company, that he was a fugitive who was armed and dangerous, and that they were offering a $25,000 reward for information leading to his apprehension."

Jason's neutral expression dissolved. "Twenty-five grand is a lot of money," he said. "They'll have people swarming all over here, playing amateur detective."

"Does this mean they've filed charges against Dane?" she asked.

"I don't know," Jason said. "We'll have to check. Is that why you're here? Because you were upset by the press conference?"

"I'm here because when I returned to my desk after the press conference, I discovered someone had cleaned it out. All my files, my office supplies and all my personal items were missing."

Jason frowned. "Did someone say something to you? Explain why that was done?"

"I didn't give them a chance. I just left. I wasn't in the mood to deal with them right now." The last thing she wanted was someone to placate—or worse—lie to her.

"Come with me to Ranger headquarters," he said. "I'll see what I can find out. And I'll let you know right away."

"All right."

It was better than sitting at home doing nothing and she wanted to believe Jason was sincere about giving her information about the case when he could. She drove behind him to the headquarters building, parked her car in a visitor's space and followed him inside just as two officers—a man and a woman—were headed out. "We've got a suspected trafficking victim over on the lake," the man, whom she recognized as Lieutenant Dance, said.

"The marina owner called it in," added the woman, Officer Redhorse, according to her name badge. "He saw one of the flyers we put up around the area."

"Good luck," Jason said, holding the door open wider to allow Cara to precede him into the office.

"Human trafficking?" she whispered as she followed him to his desk. "Here?"

"Remote areas are ideal for traffickers," Jason said. "There aren't as many people to ask questions. But it's a real concern." He nodded to a chair at one side of his desk. "You can sit while I make a few phone calls."

She sat, and he telephoned the Montrose County Sheriff's department, identified himself, and asked for any wants or warrants for Dane Trask. He put the phone on speaker so Cara could hear the response. "Trask is wanted on suspicion of fraud and embezzlement," the woman on the other end of the line said. "He's considered armed and dangerous."

Jason glanced at Cara, his gaze full of concern. She forced herself to remain steady and not give in to fear.

"Mr. Ruffino said that about Dane being dangerous at the press conference this morning," she said after Jason had ended the call.

"Does he own guns?" Jason asked.

"I don't know. I never saw him with one, but he was an Army veteran. Army Rangers. He certainly knows how to use a gun."

"He would know how to hide and how to survive in the wilderness, too," Jason said.

"I just remembered something else I thought was odd about that press conference," she said. "After saying all that about how dangerous Dane is, they didn't tell people to call the police if they saw him. They said to call a special hotline number they'd set up."

"That is a little unusual. Maybe it's something new the sheriff's department is doing. What was the number?"

She dug in the pocket of her pants and pulled out a business card. "They gave everyone who attended the press conference one of these," she said.

He took the card. Black block letters on the plain white card proclaimed:

WANTED: DANE TRASK.
6'2", 180 lbs., dark brown hair, blue eyes, 41.
$25,000 Reward for Apprehension of this
Dangerous Fugitive.
If you see him, DO NOT APPROACH.

There was a phone number. Jason took out his cell phone and punched it in. A woman's pleasant voice answered. "Do you have information about Dane Trask?" she asked.

"Who am I speaking with?" Jason asked.

"This is the hotline for information about Dane Trask. Do you have information?"

"Is this the police?" Jason asked.

"No. This is a private hotline related to the $25,000 reward we're offering for information about Dane Trask's whereabouts. Do you have information?"

"Who is running the hotline?" Jason asked.

"Do you have information about Mr. Trask?" she persisted.

He ended the call.

"A number like that is going to be inundated with false sightings, isn't it?" Cara asked. "If TDC is paying for even one person at a time to answer the phone around the clock, they're investing a lot for the slight chance that they'll be able to sift out one good piece of information from all the crackpots."

"They obviously are very interested in finding him." He tucked the card in his pocket and switched off his computer. "Did they say if he stole anything besides money?"

"No," she said. "What would he steal?"

"Valuable materials. Secrets?"

She stared at her lap, troubled by the idea. "What if he did find a secret?" she asked. "Something the company didn't want anyone else to find out about? What if they threatened him and that's why he decided to disappear?" It sounded like the plot of a detective novel, but things like that could happen, couldn't they?

"I'm not saying that couldn't happen," Jason said slowly, as if picking his words carefully. "Only that we don't have any proof that it did."

"You don't have any proof that he stole from TDC," she said. "Only their accusations."

"My job isn't to prove Dane's guilt or innocence," he said. "My job is to find him and bring him back safely."

"You may have to do the first to have any hope of the second," she said. "One thing I know about Dane—he doesn't give up. On people or ideas. It isn't in his nature. It's one of the things that makes him such a good friend."

And it would make him a formidable enemy.

Chapter Thirteen

Cara fortified herself to face whatever awaited her at TDC headquarters on Tuesday with a double cappuccino and a large blueberry muffin. She wore her sharpest suit and most comfortable dressy flats. If she ended up being escorted from the building, she didn't want to risk tripping in heels and falling on her face.

Maisie intercepted her as soon as she exited the elevator on the fifth floor. She pounced from just outside the door and seized Cara's arm. "What is going on?" Maisie demanded.

"What do you mean?" Cara eased from her friend's gasp. Had Ruffino made another announcement about Dane? Had news reporters recovered some sensationalized bit of gossip?

"Your desk is gone, that's what I mean," Maisie said. "And you weren't here yesterday afternoon. I tried calling your cell and didn't get an answer."

Cara winced. "I didn't get home until after nine and by then it was too late to call," she said, not entirely lying.

"Where were you?" Maisie asked. "I thought you were in jail or something."

"In jail?"

Maisie looked sheepish. "Well, not really. But I never thought Dane would steal a bunch of money from TDC, either."

Cara opened her mouth to protest that Dane hadn't stolen anything, but the elevator doors parted behind them and the imposing white man who had tried to take all of Dane's files emerged. "Ms. Mead," he said. "Mr. Ruffino will see you now."

Maisie gaped as the man took Cara by the arm and pulled her into the elevator. Cara thought about resisting, but how far would she get fighting off this man who outweighed her by a hundred pounds and appeared to be solid muscle? Instead, she moved as far away from him as possible in the elevator. "What does Mr. Ruffino want with me?" she asked.

"To talk." He didn't even look at her and, when the elevator opened on the top floor of the building, he stepped off without a glance back.

She could have run, but where to? And she wanted to talk to Ruffino, to demand to know what he had done with her personal belongings, and her desk. To question him about his charges against Dane.

The bodyguard—she couldn't think of him in any other way—disappeared behind a closed door and Ruffino's administrative assistant, Shara, took his place. "This way, Ms. Mead. Can I get you some coffee?"

"No, thank you." Any more caffeine and she might jitter across the floor like a wind-up toy.

Ruffino looked up as Cara stepped into his main sanctum. "Good morning, Ms. Mead. Please, sit down."

She thought about insisting on standing, then told herself she was being ridiculous and sat. She wasn't going to find out anything if she annoyed the man from the start. "Where are my things and where is my desk?" she asked.

"Your personal items have been moved to your new office," he said. "The desk is being refurbished. You'll have a new one."

Relief stole her breath and she was grateful she was sitting, her entire body felt so wobbly. Despite the cavalier attitude she had assumed, she'd been really worried about losing her job. The prospect of unemployment with a mortgage to pay had a way of doing that to a person. She cleared her throat. "What will I be doing?"

"You'll be in our data division."

She ran through her mental list of company departments. As Dane's administrative assistant, she had been part of engineering. She couldn't remember a data division. "Do you mean data processing?"

"Yes, that's it. They had an opening, and since you're no longer needed to assist Mr. Trask, we thought it would be a good fit for you."

She swallowed hard. Data processing was an entry-level position, a tedious one that involved inputting long columns of data into endless spreadsheets. It was honest, necessary work, but a job for which she was vastly overqualified. "My training is as an administrative assistant, not a data processor," she said.

"I'm sure you'll have no trouble with the new position," Ruffino said. "And in these difficult times, it's always a good idea to be flexible." His eyes met hers and she got the message he was sending: you're lucky to have a job at all, so you'd better take this one.

Gripped by the fear of failing to find another job and ending up in foreclosure, she nodded and managed to choke out, "Thank you."

"I've reviewed your employment records," Ruffino said. "You're a smart young woman. You've worked for Dane Trask for several years now."

"Yes, sir. Three years." Though if he'd reviewed her records, he already knew this.

Ruffino met and held her gaze once more. "I'm going to ask you an important question, and I want you to answer honestly. Will you do that for me?"

She nodded.

"Did you notice anything unusual about Trask's behavior in the last few weeks or months?"

"Nothing unusual."

"Nothing?"

"He worked a lot of long hours," she said. "And he seemed…preoccupied."

"Did he mention what was claiming so much of his attention? Any particular job or project that concerned him?"

"No. We…we didn't have that kind of relationship. I mean, he was my boss. He didn't confide in me."

Ruffino looked disappointed. "And you didn't observe anything particularly erratic or unstable in his behavior?"

"No." She sat straighter. Was he implying he thought

Dane was mentally ill? "Dane was the same smart, thoughtful, generous man he'd always been."

Ruffino sat back, looking pensive. "I understand."

What did he understand? She cleared her throat. "I find it hard to believe Dane would have stolen from TDC," she said. "It seems so unlike him."

"It's very natural, I believe, for a single, perhaps lonely, young woman to become enamored of a forceful, handsome man like Dane Trask," Ruffino said. "I imagine he could be very persuasive, preventing you from seeing his true nature. All the more reason to move you to a different position. One where you can make a fresh start." He stood. "I'm glad we could have this little talk."

Is that how he saw her? A pathetic, love-starved spinster, crushing on her boss? Of all the sexist clichés. She stood, trying to find words that would express her outrage but not get her fired. Before she could form a coherent sentence, the door opened behind her and the bodyguard came to stand beside her chair. "Mr. George, escort Ms. Mead to Data Processing," Ruffino said.

"I know where it is," she said and strode past George.

Unfortunately, she had to wait for the elevator and George easily caught up with her. He didn't say anything, or try to touch her, but his looming presence irritated her. As soon as the elevator door opened, she stalked off and all but ran down the hall to the data processing department. "I'm Cara Mead," she told the large woman at the first desk she saw. "I've been assigned to this department."

The woman looked Cara up and down, taking in

the purple suit and Italian leather flats. Cara was seriously overdressed for data processing. "Your desk is in the back corner," she said. "You can get started right away. Enter all the reports you find in your in-box into a single spreadsheet. If you have questions, Amy, who works next to you, will help."

Cara nodded and stalked to her desk, ignoring her coworkers. The encounter in Ruffino's office had left her hurt, insulted and afraid. Vice presidents like Mitchell Ruffino didn't single out administrative assistants like her. They didn't make a point of demoting them to data processing. Those kinds of decisions were made in human resources, or because a department head requested a particular employee.

If Ruffino had a hand in putting Cara here, was it because he deliberately wanted to insult her? Or because he wanted to keep an eye on her?

Did he think she could lead him to Dane?

"These are some of the things our campground thief has left behind. Quite a variety." National Park ranger Mike Griffen indicated the half dozen items arranged on one corner of his desk. Jason picked up a small carving of a squirrel and examined it. It was crude, but had a folk art appeal.

"The thief didn't fall for your trap, I guess," Jason said.

"Nope. He hit up a campsite right next to the blind where we were hiding. I don't see how he did it."

A former Army Ranger probably wouldn't have

much trouble outwitting most people, Jason thought. "What did he steal?"

"He took some leftover fried chicken out of a cooler in the back of a minivan and left this." Mike held up a Mont Blanc pen with a barrel that looked like polished marble.

"Nice," Jason said.

"Yeah. It's worth a lot more than the chicken he took."

"Can I borrow this to show to someone?" Jason asked.

"Do you think you know who it belongs to?" Mike asked.

"Remember the pickup we pulled out of the canyon? I think it might be the guy who owned it."

"What, he plunged into the canyon and just walked away?" Mike shook his head.

"I don't think he was in the truck when it went over," Jason said.

Mike's skeptical expression didn't fade. "And he's just hanging around the park now, living off stolen fried chicken? Why?"

"Have you heard the news reports about Dane Trask?" Prime time had been full of reports about the TDC engineer turned thief.

"The guy who stole all that money from TDC?" Mike scratched his head. "I remember now that the truck's plate was registered to him, but I didn't make the connection. That's the guy you think is stealing chicken? We've got a dangerous felon running loose near the campground and you're just now getting around to telling us?"

"I don't think he's a threat to your campers and I'm not even sure your thief is him," Jason said. "Has he approached or threatened anyone?"

"No. As far as I know, no one has even seen him. He doesn't damage anything, and he always leaves something in exchange." Mike made a face. "They're calling him the Black Canyon Bandit, like he's some folk hero or something. I heard some people are even leaving stuff out for him—cookies, beer. One guy left a grilled steak, hoping to get a souvenir, I guess. I had to threaten him with a ticket. He's lucky a bear didn't tear up his camp."

"I'll let you know if I find out anything else," Jason said. He slipped the pen into his pocket then took some photos of the other items Mike had collected from the Black Canyon Bandit's victims.

Back at Ranger headquarters, Carmen Redhorse flagged him down. "We just got a call for an agency assist over on the north rim. Want to ride along?"

"Sure." He hadn't had occasion to visit the north side of the national park since his initial orientation tour.

Jason slid into Carmen's SUV after she shifted a pile of paperwork and gear from the passenger seat. "Any progress on tracking down Dane Trask?" she asked as they headed toward the north side of the canyon along the steep rim road.

"I think he might be the person who's been stealing food from campers in the south rim campground," Jason said.

"I wondered if he was still around." Carmen ran her palms along the steering wheel. "The person I'm taking you to meet is my husband, Jake. He's a wildlife officer and he really does have a case he needs help with. But mainly, he wants to talk to you about Dane."

"You mentioned they worked together as part of the veteran's group Trask founded."

"Welcome Home Warriors. Yeah, Jake really enjoyed that. He'd like to do more, as his schedule allows. He said he had some things to tell you about Dane that might help with the investigation. But I'll let him fill you in."

"How did the two of you meet?" he asked. "Were you working a case together?"

"Not exactly." She grimaced. "I actually thought he was up to no good and tried to arrest him. Turns out he was working undercover, trying to help his family. Just goes to show first impressions aren't always correct, I guess."

For the next hour, as they made the long drive to the north side of the park, they talked about Jason's background as a park ranger and her work as one of the original Ranger Brigade members.

By the time they pulled into an overlook on the north rim, Jason was anxious to meet the man who had managed to impress this obviously not-easy-to-impress woman.

Jake Lohmiller was a lean, muscular man with close-cropped brown hair and startling blue eyes. He climbed out of his Colorado Parks and Wildlife SUV and came to meet them, grinning at his wife before turning to offer a firm handshake to Jason. "Carmen's told me a lot about you," he said. "And more about this case you're working on."

"Your wife says you know Dane Trask."

Jake nodded. "He and I worked together a couple of times on a veterans' benefit, taking disabled vets into the wilderness to fish and hike, and stuff. The work he's doing with Welcome Home Warriors is great."

"What was your impression of Trask?" Jason asked.

Jake shook his head. "When I heard he'd supposedly stolen a bunch of money from his employer, I was blown away. He just never struck me as someone who cared about money. He never talked about money, and he didn't have a flashy lifestyle. He didn't talk about traveling or expensive hobbies, and he wasn't into drugs or drinking. I can spot that kind of lifestyle a mile away."

"His admin, Cara Mead, says the same thing," Jason said. "But we both know some criminals are very, very good at hiding their crimes."

"Yeah," Jake said. "But something about this just doesn't ring true. I mean, why dump his truck into the canyon and then go on the run?"

"Because he found out TDC had learned about the embezzlement and he could be facing jail," Jason said.

"Then why continue to hang out in the area?" Jake asked. "Why not take all that money and run away to Brazil or something?"

"So what do you think is going on?" Jason asked.

"If he was the one who sent that truck into the canyon, he did it for a reason," Jake said. "Dane wasn't an impulsive guy. And he had training to survive for a long time in the wilderness."

"Jake, he's stealing tourist's fried chicken," Carmen said. "That's not exactly living on the edge."

"He's taking advantage of easy pickings," Jake said. "But I'm telling you, those Army Rangers know how to live off the land if they have to. My guess is he has snares and other supplies to allow him to stay out for a long time."

"But again, why?" Jason asked. "Why, when he has family and friends in town, and money for a lawyer to defend himself against TDC's charges? He's not going to be denied bail on an embezzlement or fraud charge. Why fake his own death and go on the run if he really is innocent?"

"If he ran, it's because he felt he didn't have any other choice," Jake said. "And he's still here because he has something to prove. He's trying to stay alive until he can stop whoever is after him."

"Why would TDC lie?" Carmen asked. "What do they have to gain by discrediting one of their own employees?"

"Maybe he found out something about one of the executives," Jake said. "Something they don't want known?"

"It's an interesting conspiracy theory," Carmen said. "But I'm not sure I'm buying it."

"You didn't know Dane," her husband said. "I do, and I'm telling you, whatever he's up to, he's got a good reason." He turned back to Jason. "I don't know if that helps you any. I just wanted you to know."

"Thanks. It gives me a little better picture of him, anyway." He took the pen from his pocket. "Do you recognize this?"

Jake studied the pen, then shook his head. "No. Is it Dane's?"

"I don't know." Jason tucked the pen away once more. "Now, what's this about a case you need help on?"

For the next fifteen minutes, they discussed the poacher Jake was trying to track, a bow hunter known for firing arrows into animals and leaving them to die. "This guy has killed six deer out of season over the past two years," Jake said. "We know it's the same guy because the arrows are all the same. And they're not cheap arrows, so he's stupid as well as wasteful. But we aren't having any luck catching him, so I'm trying to spread the word."

"We'll be on the lookout for him," Jason said.

"And I'll be looking for Trask," Jake said.

"What do you think?" Carmen asked when they were in her SUV once more, headed back to headquarters.

"I think I trust the word of a law enforcement officer more than I trust some executive I've never met," he said. "And I'm frustrated that if Dane Trask really is in trouble, he didn't turn to the police for help instead of running."

"Some people don't trust cops," she said.

People like Cara, he thought. But she needed to trust him—so that he could help Dane and so that he could be there for her.

Chapter Fourteen

Dane Trask was topic number one at TDC Enterprises these days. Around the desks in the data processing department, conversation buzzed about the reward the company had offered for Dane's apprehension, about what Dane had done with the money he'd stolen, and about what would happen to him when police finally caught him.

No one included Cara in these conversations, though she couldn't help overhearing, and she couldn't ignore the curious glances cast her way. She wanted to glare at all of them and shout that Dane was innocent, but she knew that response would only fuel more gossip.

When Maisie stopped by her desk at lunchtime on Thursday, two days after Cara had transferred to data processing, Cara wanted to leap up and hug her. As they headed together for the cafeteria, she felt like a prisoner momentarily released from her cell. "How's it going in DP?" Maisie asked, as they made their way to a back corner table.

"I'm bored out of my skull," Cara admitted.

"Are you looking for another job?" Maisie asked.

Cara knew her answer should be that she was polishing her résumé and searching for a position that made better use of her skills. But she couldn't bring herself to do that just yet. "I'm hoping Dane will come back to work and I'll get my old job back," she admitted.

Maisie's eyes widened and she leaned toward her friend and spoke in a low whisper. "Cara, honey, Dane isn't coming back. His truck crashed in Black Canyon. And if he is still alive, when they find him, he'll be in jail for a long time."

He didn't do anything wrong, Cara thought, but only pressed her lips together and shook her head. "It's surreal," she said after a moment of awkward silence. She looked down at her turkey sandwich, unable to eat another bite. "I don't believe Dane is guilty of embezzlement, and I don't believe he's dead."

"You don't believe, or you don't want to believe?" Maisie looked more concerned than sympathetic. "I'm worried about you," she added. "It's one thing to be loyal to your boss, but what you're doing goes beyond that. I mean, you're ruining your life for the guy."

"I'm not ruining my life," Cara said. "I didn't ask to be transferred to data processing. I didn't ask for people to spread nasty rumors about me and Dane."

"I was hoping you hadn't heard those," Maisie said.

"How could I not hear them? It's not like anyone is trying to keep their suspicions a secret." She shoved the uneaten sandwich aside. "So far I've heard that I'm having an affair with Dane, I'm having his baby, or I'm going to be running away to Tahiti with him." She blew out a breath in disgust. "The truth is, I haven't heard from Dane, I don't know where he is, I never dated him, and I never wanted to date him. Why can't people accept that a man and a woman who work together can be friends without being lovers?"

"Because the lovers angle makes a better story?" Maisie patted her hand. "I believe you," she said. "And I've set the gossipers straight when I get the chance, though most of them know better than to say anything to me in the first place."

"Thanks," Cara said. "That means a lot."

"Not that I'd blame you if you were into Dane," Maisie said. "I always thought he was kind of hot."

She winked, and both women burst out laughing, though there was no joy behind Cara's mirth. She just wanted this whole ordeal to be over and her life to go back to normal.

"Speaking of hot," Maisie said, looking over Cara's shoulder.

Cara turned and her breath caught when she spotted the familiar, khaki-clad figure working his way across the cafeteria. "Now there's a man you shouldn't mind spending more time with," Maisie whispered.

Jason didn't smile in greeting, but his eyes did meet Cara's with a flash of warmth. "Your supervisor said I'd find you here," he said. "Sorry to interrupt your lunch."

"I need to go for my walk now." Maisie slid out of her chair and offered it to Jason. She patted Cara's shoulder as she passed.

"I didn't mean to run your friend off," Jason said.

"It's okay." Cara tried to mean the words but she was aware of heads turned in their direction. She liked

Jason, and was even glad to see him, but word of him coming to see her would spread like a virus in a petri dish and the next thing she knew, people would be saying that she was suspected of some crime, too. "Have you found out something about Dane?" she asked.

"Is that the only reason you think I'd want to see you? To talk about the case?"

She flushed. "It's the middle of the day and we're both working. Hardly the time for a social visit."

"Fair enough." He withdrew something from his pocket and held it out to her. "Do you recognize this?"

Her breath caught as the overhead lights glinted on the barrel of the expensive pen. She knew it was expensive because she had charged the purchase to her credit card last December. "That's Dane's pen," she said. "I gave it to him for Christmas last year." She met Jason's steady gaze. "Where did you find it?"

"Someone stole some fried chicken from a camper's ice chest at the park," he said. "They left this pen in exchange."

She put a hand to her chest, her heart beating rapidly beneath her fingers. "Dane's alive. And in the park."

"It looks that way." He pocketed the pen once more.

"You need to tell Mr. Ruffino," she said. "Finding that pen means he isn't dead. You should let people know."

"And risk hordes of people descending on the park in the hope of collecting that $25,000 reward?" He shook his head.

She sagged back in her seat. She'd been so thrilled to have confirmation that Dane was alive that she hadn't considered the repercussions. He wasn't dead, but he was also a wanted man with a price on his head.

"I talked to Jake Lohmiller this morning," Jason said.

She forced herself to focus on Jason once more, and not her worries for Dane. "Who's Jake Lohmiller?"

"He's a wildlife cop, married to one of our team. He's also a friend of Dane's. They worked together with Welcome Home Warriors. He agrees with you that Dane wasn't the type to embezzle."

"It's good to know someone else is on Dane's side." She gave him a sharp look.

"I'm on the side of trying to find Dane—alive," he said. "It's up to the courts to determine guilt or innocence."

"You don't have any proof he's guilty and you have my word and the word of another cop that he's innocent. That ought to count for something."

He looked pained. "It does. But arguing Dane's guilt or innocence doesn't really help us find him."

"That pen tells you he's still in the park."

"Yes, but it's a big park. There are a lot of places for a man to hide. Especially with Dane's skills."

She straightened her shoulders. "Take me there," she said.

"Take you where? The park?"

"Yes. Take me to some of the places Dane might hide. Maybe he'll come out and talk to me."

Jason looked doubtful. "I know you don't want to believe it, but Dane might be dangerous."

"I won't believe he's dangerous to me." She gave him a pleading look. "It's worth a try, isn't it?"

"All right. When do you want to go?"

"Saturday?"

"That will work."

She stood. "I have to get back to work now."

"I'll pick you up at your house Saturday morning," he said. "We should make an early start, before it gets too hot. We should leave your place by seven."

"All right. I'll see you then."

He leaned forward and, for a moment, she thought he might kiss her—right there in front of all her coworkers. Instead, he moved back. "See you," he said, and turned and hurried away.

Back at her desk, Cara stared at the stack of statistics that needed inputting. She had never felt less motivated to do her job. Instead, she picked up the phone and punched in Audra's number.

Audra answered on the fifth ring, sounding out of breath. "Did I catch you at a bad time?" Cara asked.

"No, I was just finishing up playground duty. Now I have a couple of hours when I'm supposed to be doing paperwork." A chair squeaked and she let out a big sigh. "What's up?" she asked.

"Have you heard from the Rangers recently? Or the police?"

"A female police officer came to my office yesterday and asked me a bunch of questions about Dad—if he suddenly had a lot more money, if he was acting secretive, et cetera. I told her I hadn't noticed anything and Dad isn't one to throw money around. If anything, I think he's a little cheap. Though he'd probably say he's just not materialistic." She laughed.

"I just talked to Officer Beck, with the Rangers."

"Hud's friend. I remember."

Since when was Officer Hudson "Hud"? Cara pushed the question aside. "The Rangers don't think your father is dead," Cara said. At least, Jason didn't. "They think he's still in the park, stealing food from campers and leaving things behind in payment. He left a pen I gave him for Christmas last year."

"No one told me that! No one tells me anything."

"Cops are good about keeping families in the dark," Cara said. "I don't know if it's on purpose, or they're too busy, or they just don't think, but I've learned you have to keep after them. If you want to know anything, you have to call and ask for an update." Though even when she had done that with her brother's case, she hadn't always been able to get straight answers to her questions. At least Jason tried to be helpful.

"I don't have time for those kinds of games," Audra moaned. "I have a business to run and we're breaking ground on the new facility soon and there's just so much to deal with."

"You have a new facility? Where?"

"It's actually part of the new elementary school near the national park," Audra said.

"The one TDC is building? Dane worked on that project."

"Yes, but Dad had nothing to do with us ending up in there. The district is trying to attract and retain teachers, so they decided to offer on-site childcare and pre-school. I bid for the contract and won, so as part of the new construction, they're designing a space just for us. In addition to caring for the children of teachers, parents will be able to drop their younger kids at preschool when they deliver their older children to school. And we'll offer after-school care, as well. It's a really big deal and so exciting, and now all this with Dad—I swear, when he comes home, I'm going to give him a big hug and then I'm going to wring his neck."

"Call and talk to Officer Hudson about this," Cara urged. "I'm sure he'll fill you in."

"I will. Thanks for the heads-up. Now, I really do have to get to this paperwork."

Cara ended the call and debated dialing Eve Shea, Dane's ex-girlfriend. But she scarcely knew the woman, and she might not want to hear about Dane.

"Cara? Have you finished processing those reports?" Nina, Cara's new supervisor, loomed over the desk. Long-legged and large-chested, with a rather small head, Nina reminded Cara of a stork. Her penchant for feathered earrings didn't lessen the impression.

"Yes, ma'am." Cara would race through the stack in her in-box without bothering to try to comprehend it.

"Then if you have time for personal phone calls, you have time for another batch of reports," Nina said.

"Of course." Cara flashed a smile she hoped Nina would read as fake, but the supervisor wasn't even looking at her anymore. She was scanning Cara's desktop.

Her gaze landed on an agate paperweight and she reached over and picked it up. "This thing could be used as a weapon," she said. "Where did you get it?"

"Mr. Trask gave it to me for Christmas," she said. He had remembered purple was her favorite color, and that she was interested in geology. In that way, he'd managed to add a personal touch to a gift that was appropriate for a supervisor to give an employee.

"I'm sure you know there are some very serious charges being leveled against your former boss," Nina said.

I haven't exactly been living under a rock, Cara thought, but merely nodded.

"Some people are wondering if you had anything to do with his crimes."

This wasn't news to Cara, but having Nina come right out and say it still hurt. "If Dane did anything wrong, it was without my knowledge," she said.

"So you don't believe he's guilty?"

"I don't know what to believe, Nina." She turned toward her computer. "I just want to keep my head down and do my job."

She felt Nina's gaze on her for a long moment before the supervisor moved away. Cara looked at the paperwork and thought of Dane. Where was he right now? Did he realize how much trouble he was causing her and everyone else in his life?

"If Dane Trask is behind the petty thefts at the campground, why is he wasting our time with these games?" Commander Sanderlin addressed the team Friday morning from the head of the long conference table. "This is something the park rangers can handle. They don't need us."

"Except that Trask is a missing person who may have

been the victim of foul play," Jason said. "We can't assume he's behind the campground thefts."

"His admin identified the pen the thief left behind as belonging to Trask," Dance pointed out.

"Someone could have found that pen, and Trask's other belongings," Hud said. "They might have found Trask's body, too. We can't be sure he didn't die when his truck went into the canyon. His body might have been thrown clear."

"Knightbridge, what were the results of your campground search with Lotte yesterday afternoon?" the commander asked.

Lotte, resting on the floor next to Randall Knightbridge's chair, thumped her tail at the sound of her name. "Lotte picked up Trask's scent in the campground," the lieutenant said. "But she lost it at the creek." He shrugged. "This confirms he was there, but not where he is now. Given his military background and training, he's going to be difficult to track unless he makes a mistake.

"You're to proceed as if Trask is armed and dangerous," Sanderlin said. "We don't know why he's chosen to hide out in the park, but it speaks to a level of desperation that might lead a man to do anything."

"Tomorrow morning, I'm taking Cara Mead with me to hike near the campground and in the backcountry near there," Jason said. "She's hoping to draw Trask from hiding, since he's likely to see her as an ally."

"I'm not keen on involving a civilian in an investigation," Sanderlin said.

"That's why I wouldn't let her go on her own," Jason

said. "She could have, as someone just taking a walk in the park, and I couldn't have stopped her. I thought it was better to have someone from law enforcement with her."

"You make a good point." Sanderlin consulted his notes. "Keep me posted on your progress with the case. In the meantime, we have other business to attend to. Does anyone have any developments to report?"

"Park Service reports they stopped a man armed with a .38-caliber revolver on the Deadhorse Trail yesterday," Michael Dance reported. "He claimed not to have seen the notifications that firearms aren't allowed in the national park. Then he admitted he was searching for Trask, hoping to cash in on the reward money."

"TDC has been publicizing that reward in a big way," Carmen said. "We're probably going to see a lot more of that kind of thing as word spreads that Dane has been active in the park."

"Be extra vigilant," Sanderlin said. "We want to get to Trask before some cowboy with a gun decides to be a hero."

"I always wanted to be a hero," Hud quipped. He turned to Jason. "Isn't that why you signed up for this gig?"

"Sure," Jason said. "That and the cool uniform."

"Don't forget the chance to work outdoors in all kinds of weather and have people call you names and even shoot at you on occasion," Hud said.

"You two are a riot," Carmen said. "You ought to take your act on the road."

"Right now, you need to take it to work." Sanderlin closed his notebook and stood. "Let's get after it, people."

Hud slapped Jason on the back as they exited the room. "Come on, I want to show you something," he said.

"What is it?"

"You'll see."

They climbed into Hud's vehicle and he headed down the road to the campground and past the river crossing and the camps. After they passed the last campsite, he stopped to unlock a gate and bump down a dirt track, past a machinery shed. "Taking the scenic route, I see," Jason said.

"I think you'll find this interesting." He parked the truck when the road dead-ended and led the way down a barely discernable trail through the brush.

"Do you think Dane Trask has been down here?" Jason asked.

"I came here yesterday when I had some free time," Hud said. "I asked myself, if I'm an Army Ranger, a trained survivalist, if you will, where would I set up camp that would be convenient to the campground, yet tough for anyone to find me?"

"And your answer was here?" Jason swatted a drooping willow branch out of his way.

"It makes sense, don't you think?" Hud asked.

"I hope you're leading me down here to show me something," Jason said. "Though Trask doesn't strike me as the type to leave anything behind he doesn't want us to see."

"I agree," Hud said. "And I figure he probably knows we're looking for him."

"So?"

"So check this out." He parted a thick growth of Gambel oak to reveal a small clearing. A clearing populated with at least a dozen rock cairns. The stacks of rock had long been used as trail markers in treeless or rocky areas. More recently, however, a fad had begun of tourists leaving the rock towers on beaches, in campgrounds, and along trails, to the point where part of Jason's last jobs as a ranger in Glacier national park had been to remove the cairns that were in violation of Leave No Trace principles.

"You think Dane Trask built these?" Jason asked as he and Hud walked among the stacks of rocks, some carefully balanced creations, others more haphazardly arranged.

"I doubt random hikers ended up here," Hud said. "That trail we took in is just a faint game track. I think Trask put these here, knowing someone looking for him would eventually come across them."

"I think you're right," Jason said. He didn't have anything but intuition to back up that claim, but as a cop, he'd learned to rely on intuition more than he would ever admit out loud. "But if Trask left these for us to find, why?"

Hud shrugged. "It could be just to mess with us. Have us waste time trying to see some message where there isn't any."

"TDC is a construction company with projects all

over the world," Jason said. "Maybe these rock towers are a reference to them."

"But why?"

"I don't know." Jason squatted to take a closer look at the nearest cairn. Nine rocks of descending size, stacked one atop the other. Plain gray quartz. He picked up the top rock and held it, and thought of the piles of rocks at the Mary Lee Mine reclamation site. Were these cairns some oblique reference to that?

"We could stake out the place and hope he comes back," Hud said. "But I'm betting he won't. I wouldn't be surprised if he stopped visiting the campground. It's getting too dangerous, and I think he's smarter than that."

Jason stood. "I think you're right." He plucked the top rock from the cairn he had just examined and stuffed it in his pocket.

"What are you going to do with that?" Hud asked. "Examine it for fingerprints?"

"Just an idea I have," Jason said. He had remembered the rock Cara had collected at the Mary Lee Mine. Maybe she could help him interpret Dane's latest message.

Chapter Fifteen

Jason picked up Cara at her house at seven o'clock Saturday morning. Instead of his Ranger Brigade SUV, he drove a white Chevy pickup with an Only You Can Prevent Forest Fires bumper sticker. "You could almost pass for a Ranger," he said, surveying her khaki hiking pants and long-sleeved white shirt.

"The hat spoils it," she said, putting on a wide-brimmed straw sun hat trimmed in pink ribbon.

"I don't know," he said. "You might start a new trend. Do you think straw would suit me?"

He made a goofy face and she laughed and shook her head. "No, the Stetson suits you," she said, referring to the dun felt hat that was part of his Ranger Brigade uniform.

"If you think that's good, you should have seen me rock the Smoky Bear model," he said.

"Is that what it's called, really?" she asked.

"That's what some people call it. It's also known as a campaign hat, or the flat hat, because it has a flat brim. I still have a couple in my closet." His grin turned to a parody of a leer. "I'll have to model them for you some time."

The image of him wearing nothing but the hat warmed her through, and she quickly looked away. "Where are you taking me this morning?" she asked after a moment.

"I thought we'd hit the back country near the campgrounds, since we know Dane has been there."

"Has he taken anything else?" she asked.

"No. I think maybe it got too risky for him. That means he may have moved on to another area of the park, or even out of the park."

"I know this is a long shot," she said. "But if he is out there, I want him to see me, and to know that I'm still on his side."

"There's something else I want to show you," he said. "And see what you think."

"Something to do with Dane?"

"I'll let you be the judge of that."

He stopped for iced coffee and cinnamon buns at a drive-thru on the edge of town. "I've got some protein bars in my pack, if we get hungry later," he said, handing her one of the drinks.

"Thanks, but I've got my own emergency rations." She patted the day pack between her feet.

"Oh? What's that?"

"Snickers candy bars. I figure they're about as healthy as most energy bars, and they taste a heck of a lot better."

He laughed. "You may be on to something." They headed for the park, through cornfields and farm country, past barren ground white with alkali, then onto rolling fields of sagebrush and scatterings of cattle, their black bodies gleaming in the early morning sun. "I always imagine what it must have been like for the first peoples to see the canyon," Jason said. "Imagine riding or walking across this relatively barren landscape and coming to this massive chasm of brilliantly colored rock."

"Living so close to the canyon, I guess I take it for granted," Cara said. She stared out the window at the passing scenery. "Dane loved it there, though. He said hiking or fishing in the canyon was the one way he could truly get away from it all."

"If he spent a lot of time there, he probably knows it well," Jason said.

"He took backpacking trips into the canyon," she said. "He spent a week there once, by himself. He and Eve were still together at the time and he said she worried about him the whole time, and hated that there was no way for her to get in touch with him."

"Everything you're telling me proves it's going to be tough to locate him if he doesn't want to be found," Jason said.

He waved to the attendant at the entrance gate and turned right onto the road to the campground, a steep, curving ribbon of pavement that descended to the level of the Gunnison River and Morrow Dam. Fly fishermen waded in the sparkling water, sending graceful casts into the shadowy undergrowth or into midstream pools formed by fallen branches or boulders.

"TDC has distributed posters of Dane all over town,"

Cara said, reliving her shock at coming upon one of these flyers at the local grocery store. It featured a photo of Dane taken at the company picnic last year, and another from his official work badge. In the first, he was smiling, carefree. In the second, he wore no smile and his dark suit made him look severe, even threatening. "Soon everyone is going to know what he looks like."

"All the more reason for him to stay out of sight," Jason said.

"But why is he staying hidden?" she asked. "Why not come out and fight to prove his innocence?"

"I guess that's the big question in all of this," he said. "What's really going on?"

He parked at a locked gate past the campground and led the way along a narrow path choked in places with brush. When he stopped abruptly, Cara almost plowed into his back. "Hud showed me this yesterday afternoon," he said. "I want to know what you think."

"What am I supposed to be looking at— Oh!" Jason had stepped aside to reveal a grouping of rock towers. She had seen similar groupings before. Once when hiking Utah's canyon country and again beside high alpine lakes. Some people constructed them as works of art or as a form of meditation. Others built them to guide hikers on trails that weren't well marked. She recalled the photo in Dane's office of a grouping of such rock structures beneath a stone arch in Utah.

"Dane built these," she said. "I'm sure of it."

"Why are you sure?" he asked.

She touched the top of one structure. "They fascinated him. He took photographs of rock groupings whenever he came upon them."

"Then why did he build these?" Jason asked. "Why would a man on the run take the time to build all these cairns?"

"Because he knew someone would see them," she said. "He's trying to tell us something."

"Why be so cryptic? Why not come right out and tell us what we need to know?"

"Because he's afraid we won't believe him? Because he wants the police to discover something for themselves?" She lightly touched the top of the next cairn she passed. It didn't wobble.

"What do you think he's saying?" Jason asked.

She wished she had a quick answer for him, a solution to this whole puzzle. But her mind was blank. Did the clue lie in that photograph of the Utah cairns, now packed away in some evidence locker? "There was a photograph of cairns like these in the things from Dane's office," she said. "You should look at that."

Jason nodded. "All right. Anything else?"

She stared at the piles of rocks. Nothing about them seemed unusual or significant.

"There were piles of rocks at the Mary Lee Mine," Jason said. "Not cairns like these, but do you think he's telling us to look there?"

"Maybe?" The idea seemed far-fetched. "I tried looking at those reports again, but other than the fact that the reports show a lot of contamination, they don't tell us anything significant. The whole reason TDC is working the property is to get rid of the contamination."

"What about that rock you took from the site?" he asked.

"What rock?"

"The one you picked up just before the shooting started. I saw you put it in your pocket."

Her face burned. "It was just something to remember Dane."

"Do you still have it?"

"Of course." It was on the table in her living room. Just a yellow-gray lump of rock that didn't mean anything to anyone else.

"Do me a favor and take another look at it when you get home. Tell me if you see anything unusual about it."

"Okay." She pulled out her phone, took a few photographs of the cairns and then they walked back the way they had come. "What now?" she asked.

"We can look around more," he said. "See if you spot anything else."

She shook her head. "I don't think he's here. I don't think anyone is here."

"Then what do you want to do?"

She studied him from beneath the broad brim of her hat. "This," she said and stepped forward and kissed him.

She could tell she had caught him by surprise, but he had good reflexes and he kissed her back, arms encircling her waist as she reached up to caress his shoulders. When their hat brims collided, she tore hers from her head and let it flutter to the ground. His mouth was firm and warm against hers, his fingers kneading her hips in way that sent tension spiraling through her core.

She arched against him and felt his erection, hard and insistent.

When he finally broke the kiss, they were both breathless. He looked as dazed as she felt. "That was pretty nice," he said.

"Only *pretty*?"

"It was very nice, but I like to leave room for improvement. You know they say things get better with practice."

"*Things*? Are you always so eloquent?"

He snugged her against him once more. "All right, then. Kissing gets better with practice. And sex." He nipped at the side of her neck.

"Well, why didn't you say so?" She traced her tongue along his jaw. This felt so good. So right. Why had she waited so long to open herself up to these feelings again?

"Maybe I like to let my actions speak for themselves." He kissed her again and her body hummed with pleasure. Oh yeah, she'd been wanting this.

"This is nice, but maybe we should go somewhere more comfortable," he said.

"Mmm." She rested her head on his shoulder. "Aren't you supposed to be working?"

"Right now I'm interviewing a witness and collecting evidence."

"Is that what you're doing? Do you think you're going to find any evidence under my shirt?"

He withdrew his hand and straightened. "We probably should continue this particular investigation when

I'm off-duty," he said. "And much as I hate to see you go, I should probably take you home now."

She smoothed the collar of his uniform shirt. "All right. But why don't you come over tonight for dinner? We can discuss the case—and other things."

"I'll come prepared for an in-depth investigation." His exaggerated leer made her laugh. She couldn't remember when she'd laughed with a man this way. Not since before Corey died, surely.

That fog of happiness lasted all the way back to her house and halfway up the front walk. Then Jason stopped and pulled her back. He swore and she followed his gaze to the front door. The screen hung by one hinge and the door itself was a splintered mess. A sick feeling washed over her. "What—?" It was the only word she got out before her throat closed.

"Stay here," he said. He released his hold on her and strode toward the beat-up door. Keeping to one side, he surveyed the damage then stepped past the debris and into the house.

Less than a minute later, he joined her on the walk. "I'm going to call the local cops to handle this," he said. "We'll wait until they arrive, then you can go in and look to see what is missing."

"They took my things?" Anger pushed out some of her fear. She was almost as upset about the destroyed door as she was her belongings. She had spent a solid week stripping, sanding and repainting that door. "Was it the same scumbag who tried to break in the other night?"

"Maybe." Jason pulled out his phone. "Let's see what the local cops have to say."

A Montrose police officer arrived twenty minutes later, took a look at the splintered door and called for backup. He took their statements, including the information about the attempted break-in almost two weeks before. Then he escorted them into the house. After the destruction of the door, Cara had expected the worst, but the interior seemed undisturbed. "Tell me what's missing," the Montrose officer said.

"My laptop," she said, stomach sinking as she stared at the end of the kitchen table where the computer usually sat. She scanned the rest of the downstairs rooms. The television was still in its place, along with some other small electronics. Upstairs, all her jewelry was still there. Even the bit of cash she kept tucked in her underwear drawer was still in its envelope.

She followed the city cop and Jason back down the stairs. "Is anything else missing besides the computer?" the officer asked.

She looked around the room again, her gaze resting on the coffee table. "The rock is gone," she said.

"A rock?" The cop looked puzzled.

Cara ignored him and turned to Jason. "The rock I took from the Mary Lee Mine. It was right here on the coffee table and now it's gone."

"Was it some kind of valuable mineral specimen or something?" the officer asked.

"No, it was just a yellowish-gray lump of rock, about the size of my fist." She made a fist to demonstrate.

"It had a lot of sentimental value," Jason offered.

The cop shrugged and wrote it down. "Anything else?"

"No." Cara turned back to Jason. "Who would want my computer and that rock?"

"Come on." He put an arm around her. "Pack an overnight bag and let's go to my place. You can't stay here with the door like that."

"I can go to a hotel," she said, not enthusiastic about the prospect.

"You don't want to be alone right now."

The fact that he understood that made her feel even closer to him. While he and the Montrose officer chatted, she went upstairs and shoved some clothing and toiletries into a bag. Once downstairs again, she grabbed her phone charger from the kitchen then rejoined them in the living room. "I saw some scrap wood out back," Jason said. "If you've got a hammer and some nails, I'll seal off the doorway before we leave."

She'd been so dazed she hadn't thought of that, and was grateful he had. The Montrose officer gave her his card and a case number and told her he'd let her know if anything turned up. "You might keep an eye out online and at local pawnshops," he said. "Sometimes crime victims have better luck in tracking down their own belongings than we do."

It only took Jason about fifteen minutes to hammer a piece of plywood over the opening to the door. "The Montrose police will do extra drive-bys today and tomorrow to keep an eye on the place," he said.

"I don't think whoever did this will be back," she said. "I think he got what he wanted."

"You might be right."

Neither of them said much on the drive out toward the park. Jason turned his pickup onto a side road and wound up a hill to a log cabin in a grove of cottonwoods. "How in the world did you find this place?" she marveled as they climbed out of the vehicle.

"A ranch worker used to live in this place, but there's more gas wells than cattle on the ranch today, so the owners decided to rent it out." He took her overnight bag and led the way to the front door.

"It's certainly remote enough," she said.

"I like remote," he said. "And it's closer to Ranger headquarters and the park than I would be in town."

"There is that. It's close to TDC, too." She indicated the office complex, barely visible in the distance.

"That, too." He pushed open the door and led her into a simply furnished square room dominated by a large plate-glass window that offered a watercolor-worthy view of wildflower-covered rolling plains and distant mountains.

"Wow," she said, drawn to the window as if by suction.

"Yeah." Jason moved in behind her. "This view pretty much sold me on the place."

He wrapped his arms around her and she leaned back into him, comfortable and comforted. "I'm glad you were with me this morning," she said. "I'm glad I didn't have to deal with that by myself."

"I wish we had showed up just a little earlier and caught whoever it was in the act," he said.

She swiveled around to face him. "No one's going

to convince me this doesn't have something to do with Dane," she said. "My laptop has the files I copied from his computer on it. And that rock was from the Mary Lee Mine. It's where he's been trying to point us from the very first, I'm certain. It's one of the jobs Dane was working on before he disappeared. He must have discovered something at that mine or about it that someone else doesn't want made public. It could be the reason he felt he had to leave."

"I'm not saying you're wrong about all of that," Jason said. "But we don't have any proof."

"We need to go back up to the mine," she said. "We need to get another rock."

"And then what?" he asked.

"I don't know. We can have it tested or something."

"We could do that. And maybe this time the person who shot at us won't aim wide."

The terror of those moments under fire was still with her, so she couldn't argue with him. "Then what are we going to do?" she asked.

"I agree that Dane may be pointing us to the Mary Lee Mine. So let's take another look at that report he left on the first flash drive, and on his other files related to the Mary."

"But my computer with the files was stolen."

"But the Ranger Brigade has Dane's computer with the originals. We can go there after we have some lunch and take another look. I'll ask Hud to help us. He's our resident computer nerd."

"You don't have a resident environmental engineer, do you?" she asked. "One who can think like Dane?"

"Sorry, can't help you there." He squeezed her shoulders and stepped back. "Now, how about some lunch? I can offer you a turkey sandwich or peanut butter."

She opted for the turkey, which wasn't bad, and studied the rest of the cabin while she ate. The living room was furnished with a recliner, a sofa, a television and gaming system, and a couple of tables. The basics. A single bookshelf was crammed with paperbacks and hardbacks, everything from government reports and textbooks to bestsellers. Jason seemed to favor history and science, with a smattering of off-the-wall humor and some classics.

A dining nook sported a wooden table and chairs that looked antique, possibly original to the cabin. The kitchen was all yellow-laminate countertops and pine cabinetry, functional but not attractive enough to be dubbed retro or vintage. When she went to the bathroom to freshen up before they ate, she checked out the two bedrooms. One, obviously Jason's, held a king-size bed, a large dresser and a gun safe. The bed wasn't made but the room was otherwise neat. The second bedroom held a single bed, a chair and a lamp. The spare room of a person who didn't have company often.

"The well water here isn't that great," he said when she rejoined him in the kitchen. "So I hope you like Coke. I'm out of bottled water, so it's either that or coffee."

"Coke is fine," she said. "How long have you lived here?" she asked.

"Five weeks. I'm pretty much the newest member of the Ranger Brigade, which is why I was by myself at headquarters the afternoon you showed up to report Dane missing."

"Guess it was my lucky day," she said, flirting again, but also serious. She held her breath, waiting for his response.

"Mine, too," he said.

Happiness filled her, making her feel stupid. She was supposed to be worried about Dane, and her job, and the fact that someone had broken into her house. She needed to buy a new door, and she should really update her résumé and start looking for a new job. Yet she was helpless to do anything but sit across the table from Jason and bask in the warmth that filled her.

"When you go in to work Monday, see what you can find out about Anthony Durrell and Walter George," Jason said.

Some of the warmth faded. Apparently, he hadn't been basking in a romantic glow but had been thinking about the case. "The two men who came to my office to get Dane's computer?" she asked. "You think they're behind this break-in? Durrell is the man who was following us last Sunday night, right?"

He nodded. "I ran the names through our database, and didn't come up with anything. Which makes me suspect the names might be aliases."

"TDC requires a criminal background check on all new hires," she said.

"Maybe someone got careless. Or figured out a way around the check. All I want you to find out is how long they've worked for TDC and what their job titles are."

"You're law enforcement," she said. "Can't you call the personnel office and they have to tell you?"

"They don't have to tell me anything without a subpoena," he said.

"I'll see what I can find out," she said. "I know I never saw or heard of either one of them before they came into the office that day. TDC has hundreds of employees around the world, maybe thousands, but our office only has about a hundred, and I thought I knew, or had at least heard of, all of them. Which makes me think they were hired recently, and maybe for a very specific job."

Was the job going after Dane?

Was their job now to go after her?

Chapter Sixteen

After lunch, Jason drove Cara to Ranger Brigade head-quarters. When they entered, Hud had a rapt group of fellow Rangers gathered around him near the notice board. "When I stopped the guy and asked him what he was doing with a naked mannequin tied to the top of his car, he said it was for an art project. He couldn't transport it inside the car because he was afraid his dog would eat it."

"What kind of dog?" Knightbridge asked.

"Big. One of those big white ones you see with sheep sometimes."

"A Great Pyrenees," Carmen said.

"That's it. Anyway, I asked the guy if he could show me his project. He said sure, so I followed him to this big open field up in the high country, full of Alpine sunflowers. Just a beautiful setting." He made a face. "Except not so beautiful because this guy has, I kid you not, at least a dozen naked mannequins set up out there, posed like they're having sex. Pretty kinky sex, judging from some of the positions. I told him he couldn't do that on public land. What if some kids came along? He told me that's why he'd chosen such a remote location, and that he was very careful to clean up after himself and leave no trace. He'd been doing this for months and hadn't had any trouble."

"So he was taking pictures of the lewd mannequins?" Dance asked.

Hud nodded. "He had a whole camera full of shots—in fields of wildflowers, posed on top of rocks, in the middle of a stream—maybe fifty or a hundred different shots. He said he was going to compile them in a book."

"Did you charge him with anything?" Carmen asked.

"What was I going to charge him with?"

"Public indecency," Knightbridge said.

"These were mannequins, not real people. And it's not like they were…you know, anatomically correct."

"Littering?" Dance asked.

"It's not really littering if he takes everything with him when he leaves."

"So what did you end up doing?" Carmen asked.

"I asked him if he had considered using dolls for his project. They'd be easier to pose, cheaper to acquire, and he wouldn't freak out passing motorists if he decided to strap them to the top of his car."

"What did he think of the idea?" Knightbridge asked.

"He liked it. He said it could offer a whole new dimension to his work."

Hud was the first to notice their arrival as the group broke up. "Hey, Cara," he said. "How's it going?"

"Cara needs to take another look at Dane Trask's computer files," Jason said. "Everything to do with the

Mary Lee Mine. Start with the most recent files and move back through time."

"We can do that." Hud led them to his desk. "What are you looking for?"

"Anything in the reports that shouldn't be there," Cara said, settling into a chair beside the desk. "Or anything that should be there that isn't."

Hud settled behind the desk while Jason dragged a chair alongside Cara's. As Hud's fingers flew over the keyboard, Jason watched Cara. The break-in at her home had shaken her, but she was holding steady, thinking clearly and pushing forward. Later, the impact of her home invasion and the loss of her computer, at least, might hit harder. He hoped he could be there for her when they did.

"Okay, here are all the files having to do with the Mary Lee Mine," Hud said. "There are seventeen of them, but some appear to be memos and stuff other people sent to Trask. Do you want to look at those?"

"Yes, let's start there." Cara scooted closer. "They should be easy to scan quickly."

She dismissed the first three files. They contained emails related to the government contract and asked Dane to do a routine environmental assessment on the property showing "before" values to use as a baseline by which to judge TDC's progress with mitigation. One file contained a copy of the government's testing at the site. "Save that one to compare to Dane's initial report," Cara said, pointing to the screen.

"This looks interesting," Hud said. "Here's a file labeled 'Concerns.'" He tapped a few keys then frowned. "It's blank."

"Can you tell if it once contained something and has been erased?"

"I can try." He made a series of keystrokes, but the screen remained empty. He shook his head. "I'm not getting anything. Maybe he created the file, intending to make a list or write a memo or something, and never got around to it."

"See if you can find his initial assessment and let's compare it to the government's EPA report," Cara said.

Hud found the assessment report, opened it and displayed it next to the one from the Environmental Protection Agency. "It looks very similar," he said.

Jason scanned the list of letters and numbers, trying to remember what each one meant. "It's like the one on the flash drive," he said after a moment. "I mean, full of a lot of nasty stuff."

Cara nodded. "It is, but…" She leaned closer, scrutinizing the information. "It's what *isn't* on either of these reports that I find interesting."

Jason studied the screen again. "There's nothing on here about radioactive elements." He looked at her. "Maybe they didn't measure that initially. You said it's not common in this area. Maybe Dane uncovered it later."

"Maybe he uncovered it later because it wasn't there initially," she said.

Hud swiveled his chair to face them. "With mines, aren't we talking about naturally occurring radioactivity from uranium and other ores?"

Cara nodded. "That's my understanding. So, if it isn't there initially, how could it just show up?"

"Maybe as they started mitigating, digging out contaminated soil and rock, they uncovered some that couldn't be detected initially," Jason said.

"Maybe." She didn't sound convinced. "I've never heard of it happening. Do you have the flash drive Dane left on my car seat?"

"I have a copy of the file that was on it," Hud said. He shrank the information on the screen and brought up the fragment of the report.

"There." Cara stabbed at the screen. "There's the thorium and the uranium—radioactive elements found in soil and water."

"This report doesn't have a header, so we don't know it's from the Mary Lee Mine," Hud pointed out. "It could be from another property."

"A property that is contaminated with lead, arsenic and mercury, all by-products of gold and silver mining?" she asked.

"I would assume it's possible," Hud said. "We should find an expert to consult."

"You do that," Cara said. "In the meantime, I want to visit the Mary Lee Mine again." She turned to Jason. "Can you borrow a Geiger counter? To measure radiation?"

"It might take a little while to locate one," he said.

"Find one. Please." She rubbed her hands up and down her arms, as if chilly. "I've got a feeling we're on the right track here. Maybe the reason Dane ran was because he found the source of that radiation, and whoever was responsible threatened to kill him if he told what he knew."

"Would someone kill for that?" Hud asked.

"This remediation contract is worth a lot of money to TDC," Cara said. "The land they're trading for is potentially worth millions once it's developed. And then there's the company's reputation to consider. Bad publicity can sink stock shares, reduce executive compensation and stockholder dividends and, if it's bad enough, destroy the company."

"Some people will go to great lengths to protect their money and their reputations," Jason said.

Cara nodded. "But who? Charles Terrell, Gary Davis and Drew Compton? Mitchell Ruffino? Or someone else?"

After putting in a few calls to try to obtain a Geiger counter or some other instrument to measure radiation, Jason took Cara back to his place. He took a mental inventory of the contents of his refrigerator and pantry and realized the cupboard was all but bare. "I'm going to run to town for some groceries," he told her. "Why don't you relax? Make yourself at home."

He headed to the nearest grocery store and hurried through, filling his cart with ingredients for salad, fruit, fresh bread, half-and-half, butter, cheese, a bottle of wine—another bottle of wine in case Cara didn't like the first one—bagels, bacon, steak, potatoes, trail mix, bottled water, cereal, milk and a big chocolate bar. Surely he could come up with a couple of decent meals from all this, enough to take them through tonight and tomorrow morning.

When he stepped through the door, the first thing he noticed was that Cara's overnight bag was no longer where he had left it—and she wasn't anywhere to be seen.

He'd left her bag by the front door, leaving it to her to decide which room she wanted to sleep in. He knew what he wanted, but she was calling the shots.

"Cara?" he called as he carried the groceries to the kitchen.

"I'm back here!"

He shoved the bags full of cold items onto the top shelf of the refrigerator and went in search of her. "Back where?"

"Back here!"

He thought the voice was coming from his bedroom. As he pushed open the door, his heartbeat sped up a little then did gymnastics as he stared at Cara, wearing a little—very little—nightie, sitting in the middle of his bed. "I didn't really feel like resting," she said. "And I thought maybe dinner could wait."

Between the door and the bed, he managed to lose his shoes, duty belt and pager, and was fumbling with the buttons on his shirt when she leaned back, smiling. "Don't be in a hurry on my account," she said.

"Then I'll be in a hurry on my account." Aware of her gaze on him like a caress, teasing every nerve ending and heating his skin, he managed to strip off the rest of his clothes efficiently if not gracefully. When he was naked, he turned to face her.

She stretched out her arms. "Welcome home."

The words had never sounded more inviting.

PART OF CARA had died right along with her brother—the carefree part of her. The part of her willing to trust and take life as it came. It wasn't that she couldn't have fun after Corey's death, but she did so with a hyperawareness of how good things could turn bad in an instant.

Jason helped her forget that. In his arms, she felt guilt and regret and fear falling away as easily as the silk nightgown slid from her shoulders to the floor. He loved her with a focus and intensity that compelled her to put everything else to the side. As his hands and lips moved over her, she surrendered to pleasure, so intense it made her cry out, not with pain, but with delight.

Though he devoted himself to her pleasure, he asked the same of her, guiding her hands to touch him in ways that made him groan with need, coaxing her to move with him until they balanced on the edge of completion.

Then he cradled her to him and took her over the edge, her climax shuddering through them both. He followed and they continued to move together until they were utterly spent and sated.

They didn't talk much afterward. She didn't have words to express what she was feeling. Maybe he felt the same way. But he continued to hold and caress her—as if she was something precious he didn't want to let go of—until she fell into a deep sleep. She didn't dream. Maybe because their lovemaking had been so dreamlike in itself.

SHE WOKE TO the smell of sizzling steak and her mouth began to water even before she pulled on his shirt as a makeshift robe and made her way, barefoot, to the kitchen. Jason, in a blue-velour bathrobe, his hair sticking up on one side, stood at the stove, frying steaks in a cast-iron skillet. "That smells like heaven," she said.

Before Cara could protest that she hadn't brushed her teeth or combed her hair, he pulled her to him and kissed her, still holding a spatula in his free hand. "I was starved," he said. He nodded to the sink. "If you want to help, there's stuff for a salad over there."

She washed her hands and went to work tearing lettuce and chopping vegetables. He pulled a loaf of bread from the oven, filling the room with the scent of garlic and butter, then filled two glasses from a bottle of wine that sat open in the center of the table.

"Dinner is served," he announced.

She checked the clock on the stove—only a little after eight. She hadn't slept all that long, after all, but she felt revived. "I could get used to this," she said. "You're a pretty good cook."

"No I'm not." Jason cut into his steak. "I know how to do steak, pork chops, hamburgers and eggs. I can make a sandwich and open a can of soup. I don't starve, but don't go thinking I'm a real chef."

"I do a mean macaroni and cheese and spaghetti Bolognese," she said. "Oh, and meat loaf. I can do meat loaf. And I can read and follow most recipes. It's just that, when you're only cooking for yourself, there's not much incentive to get creative. Most days when I get home from work, I just need food, fast."

"Exactly." He stabbed at the salad with a fork. "It's kind of fun to cook for someone else."

"How old are you?" she asked, feeling emboldened—

by the sex or the wine or maybe the fact that she was sitting across from him, naked under his shirt and not even shy about it.

"I'm twenty-nine," he said. "Why? How old are you?"

"I'm thirty," she said. "And why? Because you sound like you've managed to reach twenty-nine without ever being married. Is that true?"

"That's not really so unusual these days, is it?" he said. "I've never even lived with anyone, either. What about you?"

She shook her head. As long as they were confessing their pasts, she might as well lay it all out on the table. "I was engaged to a guy when Corey died. We weren't living together. I mean, we were lovers, but I wanted to save something for after the wedding. But I kind of fell apart after Corey's death and my fiancé wasn't the most patient guy." She shrugged. "I gave back his ring, sold the dress online and told myself I was lucky to find out what he was really like before I vowed 'till death do us part.'"

"What a jerk."

She laughed, covering her mouth with her hand to avoid spraying salad across the table. "When you put it that way, he really was," she said. She sipped the wine, then pointed her fork at him. "Your turn. What's your bad relationship story?"

He made a face. "She was a congressional staffer for a freshman representative. We met at a press conference on the steps of the House of Representatives. I was working crowd control and I didn't want to let her onto the dais. She didn't have her ID badge with her and pitched a fit. She read me the riot act and I asked her out."

"You didn't!"

He shrugged. "What can I say? I like strong women. Anyway, things were great for a while, but, as the saying goes, we grew apart."

"Oh?"

"She was ambitious. And she was really into politics. I'm not either of those things. I aim to do a good job, but I don't see myself as commander one day, and I'd rather have a root canal than talk politics, much less wade into the nitty-gritty. When I refused to attend yet another fundraising dinner for her boss, we agreed to go our separate ways."

"That was very mature of you."

"Oh sure. Very mature. I didn't date anyone else for over a year."

"She broke your heart."

He shook his head. "I just felt stupid for getting involved with someone I knew was wrong for me from the start. I got a lot pickier after that. For a while, I was thinking I was too picky."

Cara pretended to focus on finding the tomatoes in her salad. "What happened to change your mind?"

"I met you."

Her heart skipped a beat and a knot formed in her throat. It wasn't exactly a dramatic declaration of love, but the words weren't idle flirtation, either. "Do you think we have more in common than this case?" she asked.

"I think we both value the same things—family, loyalty, fairness."

"Truth, justice and the American way."

She regretted the quip as soon as it was out of her mouth, but he had the grace to let it pass. "I think it's worth finding out how much we have in common," he said. "And what we can gain from our differences. For instance, do you prefer to wash or dry?"

"Dry," she said.

"That's interesting," he said. "I prefer to wash."

"Then we are a perfect pair."

Cara never would have believed washing dishes could be romantic, but with her standing barefoot in his kitchen—the sleeves on his uniform shirt rolled up to her elbows, the scent of him clinging to the fabric— and him in his bathrobe—strong legs distracting her every time he stepped away to take another dirty dish from the table— the mundane chore was both sensual and intimate.

When the last dish was done, Jason turned to her, pressing her against the counter and kissing her, his hands deftly unbuttoning the shirt and pushing it back to expose her body. She parted his robe and they came together, the need sharp and demanding, until he lifted her onto the counter and bent his head to kiss and tease between her legs until she came with a loud cry.

Then he carried her over his shoulder to the bedroom, her laughter trailing them down the hall, a joyful sound. One she hadn't been sure she would ever make again.

"WHAT DID YOU do last night?" Hud asked when Jason reported for work on Monday morning. "You look hung over."

Jason shook his head. "I had an early night," he said. Though, if it were possible to suffer from overindulging in sex, then maybe that was his problem, since most of the weekend had been spent in bed.

He'd say one thing for Cara—when she finally decided to do something, she gave it one hundred percent. He shouldn't have been surprised. She'd been dogged in her determination to save Dane. She had probably been the same after her brother died, wanting justice for him so desperately.

Jason didn't know if the Houston cops had really blown her off, as she'd said, or if it only seemed that way. Like so many law enforcement agencies, the department was likely understaffed, underbudgeted, overworked and overwhelmed by all the ways people found to break laws and hurt each other.

He would do his best not to hurt her. To find Dane and either bring him to justice or help him find it. The deeper he delved into the case, the more he tended to believe Cara—the man was running from something. Something to do with his job. Whether that was because he had stolen money, or because he harbored a secret someone didn't want exposed, Jason couldn't say.

"The Department of the Interior says they have a Geiger counter you can borrow," Dance called from across the room. "Somebody left a message in our voice-mail box."

"What do you need a Geiger counter for?" Knight-bridge asked.

"I'm looking for radioactive material that shouldn't really be at a mine TDC Enterprises is supposed to be cleaning up," Jason said. "It showed up on an environmental impact report and I'm trying to find the source."

"I thought you were working on the missing Dane Trask case," Dance said.

"I am," Jason said. "This is related."

"If you say so." Dance turned his attention back to his computer screen.

"Black Canyon staff say no more reports of thefts from the campground," Carmen said. "Maybe the thief has moved on."

"Or maybe he's dead."

Every head in the room turned to the speaker, Special Agent Ethan Reynolds, another Ranger Brigade veteran. "It's rough country out there," Reynolds said. "One wrong move and you've fallen and cracked your head. Or worse, you're hurt, no one knows, and you lie there until you succumb to your injuries. It's ugly but it happens."

"Trask was a former Army Ranger," Jason said. "He had a lot more training than your average tourist. And he was familiar with the area. He'd spent a lot of time hiking and camping in the canyon and the wilderness areas over the years."

"Then maybe he's still alive and headed for Mexico," Reynolds said. "Or Santo Domingo or Alaska. There are a lot of places for a resourceful person to disappear."

"Missing person cases are the worst," Knightbridge

said. "Even if you do find the person alive, someone is going to be hurt because they left."

They filed into the conference room for morning roll call. Commander Sanderlin greeted them by name as he moved toward the front of the room. "We've got orders from Washington to make the Dane Trask search a priority," he said without further preamble. "Because this was his last-known location, we're going to divide the park into quadrants and search in teams. If we don't locate him there, we'll expand to the surrounding public lands. The Montrose County Sheriff's Office will also be conducting searches in their jurisdiction."

"Why the priority?" Jason asked. *And why orders from Washington?* he wondered silently.

"It turns out Trask is accused not only of embezzling from his employer, he may be in possession of material that could endanger national security," Sanderlin said.

"What material?" Knightbridge asked.

The commander frowned. "I pressed for the same information. My supervisors were reluctant to elaborate, but they implied Trask has nuclear material that could be used to construct a bomb."

"Maybe that explains the radiation in those reports," Hud said.

As far as Jason was concerned, it didn't explain anything. "So he's just carrying this stuff around in his backpack?" he asked.

"I don't know the answer to that, but he's considered armed and extremely dangerous," Sanderlin said.

Clearly, they weren't getting the whole picture here. Nothing new where the Washington bureaucracy was concerned. Jason forced himself to sit back in his chair and remain calm. More people searching for Trask was a good thing. They were more likely to find him this way. More likely to hear his side of the story when they did.

"You should also know that the sheriff's department expects to make another arrest in the case today." Sanderlin's eyes met Jason's, steady and serious. "Cara Mead is suspected of assisting Trask with the theft of the material. Federal authorities will be picking her up ASAP and holding her for questioning."

Chapter Seventeen

Cara dreaded walking into work Monday morning. She used to be proud of working for TDC, a company known for treating its employees well. She believed the work she and Dane did helped to protect the environment. TDC had won architectural awards for some of its buildings, and developed new techniques for building greener structures.

Yet she was convinced that something had happened here that had driven Dane to escape to the wilderness. And that same something had led to her being demoted and her house burgled.

She wasn't going to sit around and let them run her off the way they had Dane. She had a plan. Today, she was going to find Durrell and George. And she wasn't just going to give the information to Jason. She was going to confront Durrell about seeing him following her. He'd probably tell her some lie, but at least she would have alerted him that she was on to him, and that she wasn't going to let him get away with that kind of harassment.

She had spent the drive to work coming up with

a plausible story to ferret the information she needed out of human resources. As soon as she had stowed her purse in her desk, she gathered up a stack of print-outs, stuffed them in a file folder and headed for the HR department.

Donna Lapinski, six foot two in towering heels, with shoulders so broad she probably had to have her suit jackets custom tailored, greeted Cara with a warm smile. "Cara! I haven't seen you in ages," she declared. "How are you doing?"

"I'm fine," Cara lied. "I guess you know I'm in data processing now. I'm looking for an Anthony Durrell. A new employee, I guess. I've never heard of him."

Donna's brow furrowed beneath her fluff of bangs. "I don't remember anyone by that name, but let me check." She turned to her computer and began typing. After several minutes, her frown deepening, she shook her head. "I'm not finding anyone by that name. Are you sure that's right?"

The hair at the back of Cara's neck stood up. "How about Walter George?" she asked.

A new search didn't turn up George, either. "I'm sorry," Donna said, looking truly regretful. "Maybe double-check that you have the right names."

"I'll do that. Thanks."

Cara turned to make her way back to her desk, un-nerved by the encounter. When they had come to Dane's office, Durrell and George had definitely worn TDC ID badges. Had the badges been fakes?

She had just stepped onto the elevator when her cell phone buzzed. She didn't recognize the number but she smiled when she saw the text was from Jason. But her smile changed to dismay when she read his message.

Get out of the building now! he had typed. Run!!

JASON HIT SEND on the throwaway phone someone—he suspected Hud, but couldn't be sure—had left on his desk after the commander had made his announcement regarding Cara. He had stared at the phone for approximately fifteen seconds before sliding it into his pocket, grabbing his day pack and heading out the door.

He didn't want to think about the laws and regulations he had just broken by trying to warn Cara of her imminent arrest. Maybe the sheriff's office, or Homeland Security, or whomever was involved in this case had come up with evidence to indicate Cara was implicit in a plot to steal radioactive material and sell it to terrorist groups or foreign agents or something like that. But he didn't believe it. And nothing he had seen of Dane Trask and his background pointed to his guilt, either.

But Cara was the only person Jason cared about. And he was starting to care very deeply. After so many years of guarding his heart, he'd opened up wide to her. If she ended up in prison, he would feel like he was there, too.

He headed for TDC headquarters. To do what, he didn't know. Maybe only to be there when federal agents hauled her away, to let her know he was there for her. He circled the employee parking lot in his Brigade SUV, searching for her car. He didn't see it on the first pass, but as he turned back into the lot for another look, two Montrose County Sheriff's Office vehicles and two plain black SUVs drove in from the front of the building.

Just then, Jason spotted Cara exiting the building. She walked rapidly toward a back corner of the lot. He sped toward her, putting his vehicle between her and the law enforcement SUVs, which were still on the far side of the lot. At his approach, she whipped her head around, her expression rigid with fear.

Relief, coupled with confusion, relaxed her features as she recognized him. She jogged to the passenger's-side door and yanked it open. "Get in the back," he said. "And get down, so no one can see you. I'll explain later."

She hesitated only a moment, then climbed into the back and got down on the floor. He reached back, pulled a blanket from a side pocket and draped it over her, then proceeded out of the lot. As he passed the first sheriff's department vehicle, he lifted one finger in salute. The officer at the wheel returned the greeting, and Jason proceeded past the others in the party, back onto the highway, where he pushed the Cruiser up to eighty, headed toward the lake.

"Where are we going?" Cara asked, her voice muffled by the blanket.

"I'm going to drive out to the Curecanti wilderness area. Once we're on the backroads, it should be safe for you to sit up."

"What's going on?" she asked. "Am I in some kind of danger?"

"Maybe. I'll tell you what I know when we're stopped." He wanted to look into her eyes when he told her the news, to see for himself that she was innocent.

He drove for another fifteen minutes before he turned off on a side road that led through a state wildlife area and into the national forest, all part of the Curecanti National Recreation Area, and part of the Ranger Brigade's jurisdiction. "You can sit up now," he told Cara. "I'll stop and we'll talk when we get to some trees."

She sat up and he glanced in the rearview mirror to watch her. Hair mussed and face flushed, she snapped in her seat belt and stared out the side window, her expression troubled. But she didn't ask any more questions. Maybe that was a sign that she trusted him to tell her the truth when the time came.

After bumping over the narrow, rutted road for another ten minutes, Jason turned onto a barely discernable dirt track, even rougher and rockier than the forest road on which they'd been traveling. "This looks like the kind of place where serial killers dispose of bodies," Cara said. "Though, if that's what you have planned for me, you certainly have a unique abduction method. I didn't know what to think when I got your text."

"But you paid attention and left," he said. "Thank you for that."

"I figured you wouldn't have sounded so urgent if you hadn't had a good reason. It confused me that the message wasn't from your phone, though."

"I had to use a phone no one could trace."

She leaned forward, grasping the back of the seat. "What's going on? You're starting to scare me."

He pulled over in the shade of a lone oak, rolled down the windows and shut off the engine. The only sounds were the wind's rustling of the leaves of the tree and the ping of the cooling engine. "Come up here," he said.

She got out of the back and transferred to the front passenger seat. "Did you see the sheriff's department vehicles drive into the parking lot, just when you came out of the building?" he asked.

She shook her head. "I was focused on getting to my car. Your message really scared me. Why did I need to leave?"

"They were coming to arrest you."

All color left her face. "Arrest me? For what?"

"For conspiring with Dane Trask to steal nuclear material—and other potential terrorist activities."

"Terrorist activities?" She pressed a hand to her stomach. "I feel sick."

He retrieved a bottle of water from a small cooler on the floorboard of the back seat and handed it to her. "I don't know much," he said. "My commander announced that you were going to be arrested at the end of our morning meeting. We've had orders from Washington to beef up the manhunt for Trask. I'll have to get back soon to help with that."

"I'm not a terrorist," she said. "And neither is Dane. What proof could they possibly have of anything like that?"

"I don't know," Jason said. "But it may have something to do with the radioactivity on those reports for the Mary Lee Mine."

Cara sank back in the seat and closed her eyes. He reached over and took her hand and, for a moment, neither said anything, soaking in the quiet and calm. After a long while, she opened her eyes. "Thank you for text-ing me," she said. "I know you didn't have to do that. You could probably lose your job if anyone finds out you helped me."

"Probably," he agreed.

"So why did you?"

He opened his mouth to say something flippant and flirtatious—he hadn't had a chance yet to taste her fa-mous meat loaf or he'd decided to take more chances in his life. But what came out was the truth. "Because I think I'm falling in love with you. And because I be-lieve you're innocent."

Tears glistened in her eyes—not the reaction he had expected or particularly wanted. "What's wrong?" he asked. "Did I say the wrong thing?"

"No." She shook her head and dabbed at her eyes. "You said exactly the right thing. But what are we going to do?" She looked around. "I left work so fast, I didn't even grab my purse. Do you have a tissue?"

He had a box in the console and handed it to her. She wiped her eyes and blew her nose. "When I got your message, I'd just left the human resources department," she said. "I asked about Anthony Durrell and Walter George. The HR director had never heard of them, and she couldn't find them on her computer."

"At this point, I'm not surprised," he said. "Nothing about this case adds up."

"What are we going to do? When the sheriff doesn't find me at TDC, he'll go to my house. He may even go to your house."

"I agree. For whatever reason, TDC, or someone

else, is very serious about stopping you and Trask. We need to find that reason."

"We need to go back to the Mary Lee Mine," she said.

"I don't have a Geiger counter," he said. "I've found someplace that will loan me one, but I have to go pick it up, and I doubt I can get to that today."

"I still think we need to go to the mine," she said. "I can take water and soil samples and send them off for testing. I used to mail off samples like that for Dane. I can make up a fake name."

"That takes time," Jason said. "I don't know how long I can keep you hidden."

"I feel terrible involving you in all of this," Cara said.

"I'm in now," he said. "And I'm not going to make you go through this by yourself."

She dabbed at her eyes again. "You have to stop that. I'm ruining my makeup."

"Stop what?"

"Saying such sweet things."

He leaned forward and kissed her—a gentle caress, meant to be reassuring. She clung to him a moment before letting go. His arms felt empty without her in them. He used to laugh when people—his family, usually—said one day he'd want to settle down. He liked living different places, making friends all over the world. Everywhere he'd lived—Ghana, Glacier, Washington, DC—he'd had women in his life. They'd all been special to him, but he had never had a problem moving on. Cara felt different. She felt like someone he couldn't move on from. Someone he couldn't afford to lose.

"You need to get back to work," she said. "I don't want them to arrest you, too."

He started the SUV's engine. "I'm going to drop you off at a place where I think you'll be safe," he said. "At least for a few hours. I don't know how long I'll be on search duty, but when I get a break, we'll go up to the Mary Lee Mine. Promise you'll wait for me and won't try to go alone."

"I won't," she said. "Maybe a week ago, I would have. But you have a gun and I don't, and we may need one."

"So you just love me for my weapons."

"Oh yeah," she said. "I love a man who's armed and dangerous." She squeezed his arm, adding meaning to the teasing words. "If you're not careful, I'm going to start to rely on you."

"I think I can handle that if you can."

"You've got me thinking differently about a lot of things."

He hoped the future—their future—was one of the things she was thinking about. But maybe it was too soon for that. They wouldn't have any kind of future if they didn't deal with the danger in the present.

THE HIDEOUT JASON had in mind proved to be a rustic log cabin nestled in a hollow of land overlooking the Blue Mesa Reservoir. Constructed of weatherworn chinked logs, the cabin consisted of only one room and an outhouse. "Who owns this place?" Cara asked, as he reached up under the eaves and took down a brass key to unlock the door.

"It belongs to a friend I worked with at Glacier National Park. When he found out I was transferred here, he told me I could use the place anytime I wanted. It's been in his family for years, but they don't make it out here much."

The furnishings inside were stark: a double bed in one corner, an antique gas stove in the other, a metal sink, a table and a few chairs, and bare shelves that held a few ancient-looking canned goods. "I'll stop on my way back for some groceries and things," Jason said, setting half a case of bottled water, a can of roasted peanuts and some protein bars he'd taken from his vehicle on the table.

She walked to the window and looked out over the turquoise waters of Blue Mesa Reservoir. Sunlight sparkled on the choppy surface and boats darted about like water bugs. "No one will think to look for me here," she said.

Jason moved in behind her and squeezed her shoulders. "I'll leave the throwaway phone with you. If you need to call me, use it."

She leaned back against him, still not quite believing he was taking such a big risk to help her. In his position, she wasn't sure she would have had the courage to do the same. "Thank you," she said.

"You don't have to thank me," he said.

"I do." She turned to him. "I say it to remind myself how lucky I am." She pulled his mouth down to hers and kissed him as if it was the last chance she'd ever get to do so. She didn't want to believe that might be true, but a panicked voice inside her whispered it might.

He broke the kiss, reluctantly, she thought. "I don't know how long I'll be gone," he said. "We're supposed to start the search in the national park. If they move it outside the park, you'll have to move. This cabin won't be safe anymore."

"Maybe I won't need to hide by then." Maybe they'd find something to help prove she was innocent. That Dane was innocent.

After Jason left, Cara stood for a long time at the window, the sun hot on her face. She could make out people on some of the boats, probably having the time of their lives racing across the water. If someone came for her here, should she run for the water or for the hills? She wasn't Dane. She didn't know anything about surviving in the wilderness.

So should she surrender and take her chances at proving her innocence? Jason apparently didn't see that as an option. He hadn't even suggested it. Maybe because he sensed, as did she, that evidence didn't have much to do with the accusations being made against her.

She sat on the bed, which squeaked loudly in protest, and picked up the little pay-as-you-go phone Jason had left for her. She punched in Maisie's number and listened to it ring.

Her friend answered on the third ring. "Hello?" She sounded doubtful.

"Don't hang up," Cara said. "It's me."

"Cara!" Maisie lowered her voice to a strained whisper. "Where are you? There were cops here, looking for you. What is going on?"

"I haven't done anything wrong," Cara said. "But listen, I need you to do something for me."

"What is it?"

At least she hadn't outright refused. "I need you to scan me copies of the forms to submit environmental samples to our lab," Cara said. "You can send them to this number."

"Lab forms? What for?"

"I need to send in some soil and water samples."

"You're still concerned about your job when you have the cops after you? Cara, I don't even know if you have a job anymore. Your supervisor almost fainted when six big guys in uniform—six!—walked into her office and asked to see you. I had come down to ask if you wanted to have lunch later and saw them. It's like they thought you were dangerous or something."

"What am I supposed to have done?" Cara asked.

"They said it related to national security. Do they mean, like, terrorism?"

"I'm not a terrorist," Cara said.

"Of course you're not. But what's going on?"

"When I figure that out, I'll let you know."

"Some of the girls are saying you must be guilty because you ran," Maisie said.

"I'm not guilty," Cara said. "But I am afraid."

"Oh, honey! I'm so sorry. I wish there was something I could do to help."

The sympathy in Maisie's voice made Cara's chest feel tight. "Just send those forms, okay? Now I'd better get off the phone."

"Wait, where—?"

Cara ended the call. She hoped she hadn't already talked too long, that the Feds or whomever was after her hadn't tapped Maisie's phone, or whatever they did with cell phones. Just in case, she shut off the phone and returned to looking out the window.

Dane, where are you? she thought. *If I could talk to you, would you tell me what's really going on?*

Had Dane run because, like her, he was suddenly afraid for his life?

Chapter Eighteen

Jason and Hud were assigned to search terrain north and east of the North Vista Trail, at the far reaches of North Rim Road. The area was less than a mile, traveling down the canyon, from the place where Dane's wrecked truck had been found. The two positioned themselves thirty feet apart and began walking forward, planning to cover the entire area in a grid pattern, bushwhacking through thick undergrowth, alert for footprints or clothing fibers, or any sign their fugitive might have passed this way.

It took four hours to all but crawl across the entire search area. By the time they were done, they were hot, thirsty, bruised and scratched, and thoroughly annoyed. "This is nuts," Hud said as they regrouped beneath the shade of the overhanging canyon walls. "If this guy stole a hundred thousand dollars or whatever it was, he's not sweating down here in this canyon. He's taking it easy on a beach somewhere."

"He's supposed to be on the run with 'nuclear material.'" Jason put verbal quotation marks around the words.

"Right—he's hiking around with a few pounds of yellowcake in his backpack? Can't that stuff give you cancer or make your hair fall out or something?" Hud stowed his water bottle back in his pack. "I've spent a lot of time going through Trask's files and he strikes me as a lot smarter than that. He's a scientist, not some ignorant yahoo with an urge to overthrow the government."

Jason took off his hat and mopped his brow with the sleeve of his uniform shirt. "Then why are we out here hunting him?"

"Because somebody has evidence we don't know about?" Hud sounded doubtful. "The commander doesn't like it, either, I don't think. I could tell by the way his lip curled when he said the order came down from Washington." He kicked at a rock. "We've got better things to do than try to search every inch of the park. It can't be done, even if we had five times the staff."

"Then why are we out here?" Jason asked again.

"I think we're making a show to satisfy the higher-ups. After a day or two with no result, they'll leave us alone to go back to our real jobs."

"Maybe," Jason said. He didn't believe it. Someone was putting a lot of pressure on someone else to find Dane Trask.

"I was pretty shocked to hear that about Cara Mead," Hud said. "About her being wanted as Trask's accomplice. She seems like a really nice woman."

"Yeah," Jason agreed, wary of showing too much enthusiasm. For Cara's safety, he needed to keep quiet about their relationship.

"I guess by now they have her in custody. I hope she's got a good lawyer."

"Uh-huh."

"What's with you?" Hud asked. "You're not much of a conversationalist this afternoon."

"I'm just tired." Jason replaced his hat and straightened. "Come on. Let's search our next coordinates."

Hud took out the map and indicated a section outlined in yellow highlighter. "This one here. There're some caves in the sides of the cliff we should check out."

"Did you bring any bear spray?" Jason asked.

Hud made a face. "Have you ever seen a bear down here?"

"No, but the park rangers say they're down here."

"If we run into any, I'll fire my sidearm to frighten them away."

"I'm not worried about black bears," Jason said.

"Why not?"

"Because I'm pretty sure I can run faster than you."

Hud laughed, breaking some of the tension, and they continued their search. Jason scanned the ground, a mix of dry, sandy earth and crumbled shale, pockmarked from past rainstorms. It was good soil for tracking because it held every imprint in the brittle surface. Everywhere he stepped, he left a clear outline of his boot, right down to the logo, on the soil.

Trask wouldn't have walked here. He'd have stuck to the rocks along the canyon wall, the rough, granite surface leaving no trace of his passage.

Determined not to waste any more time with busywork, Jason moved over toward the canyon walls. He wasn't a trained tracker, but he'd spent enough time hunting that he'd learned to read signs. Trask wasn't going to be careless enough to leave anything obvious, but it was tough for a big man like him to move through dense brush without leaving some kind of evidence behind.

His first indication that someone had been this way was a bit of lichen torn from the surface of a boulder. The bright orange growth had been smeared across the granite, just a faint smudge, possibly made by a boot slipping on the surface of the rock.

Farther on, he noted the broken tip of a stunted juniper, the end dangling where something—or someone—had brushed past.

Jason almost stumbled into the rock cairns. Three of them, one facing the other two, as if in a standoff. A chill swept over him as he surveyed the image and goose bumps rose on his arm. "Dane Trask!" he shouted.

Dane Trask! The words echoed back to him, the sound hollow and distorted.

Jason turned in a slow circle, until his eyes ached from staring, unblinking. Trask was somewhere nearby. The message of the cairns had been clear as spring water: I see you.

CARA FILLED OUT the forms Maisie had forwarded, with the location of where the sample was taken and the person the information was to be sent to. She used the name of a woman who used to work in the environmental engineering department, one who would be familiar to anyone at the lab who had worked with TDC samples before. She left the time and date the sample was taken blank, along with the address the results should be sent to. Later on, she'd print out the forms and fill in the blanks, then mail them off with the samples from the Mary Lee Mine.

Now all she had to do was wait for Jason to return so they could go to the mine. She still couldn't believe she and a cop were working together. If they weren't actually breaking the law, they were bending it pretty significantly. But what choice did they have? She'd never been a fan of conspiracy theories, yet right now it felt as if she was in the middle of a big one.

Paperwork done, she had nothing to occupy her. She toured the cabin, which took less than five minutes, including opening every kitchen drawer and checking under the bed. She had already viewed the outhouse, a dark, dry space inhabited by spiders and dust.

She lay down on the bed, too nervous to sleep, and studied the board-and-batten ceiling. The sound of tires on gravel made her bolt upright, heart pounding so hard it hurt. When she recognized Jason's pickup outside, she almost collapsed in relief.

A few seconds later, he came in, carrying plastic grocery bags and a paper sack from a local hamburger place. He set them on the table. "I got a cooler and some ice, too," he said. "I realized this place doesn't have a refrigerator."

"How long do you think I'll have to stay here?" Cara asked, surveying all the food she was too nervous to eat.

"I don't know."

"I want to head up to the mine while we still have light," she said.

"All right. Let's pack food to take with us."

She started to protest, but he silenced her with a look. "You may not want to eat, but you have to."

"Yes, sir."

He smirked and went out to retrieve the ice.

The sight of the Snickers bar among the groceries brought a lump to her throat. It was such a stupid little thing, but she was beyond touched that he had remembered.

"What happened today?" she asked as they put the burgers and fries in the backpack.

"Hud and I spent the afternoon bushwhacking through oak brush and cactus. We didn't see anything but one skinny coyote and a bunch of rocks." He glanced at her. "I think Dane was out there, though. I think he knew we were looking for him."

"What makes you think that?"

"I found three more of those rock cairns. Like, one for him and one for each of us. They were arranged in a kind of standoff. I think he was saying he wasn't afraid. That he wouldn't let us catch him."

"This isn't a game," she said, frustration making her words sharper than she had intended.

"I know that," he said, his voice gentle.

"I'm not upset with you—I'm upset with Dane. If he knew you were there, why didn't he just speak to you? Why all these cryptic clues and hide-and-seek?"

"Maybe he doesn't trust cops. There are people like that, you know."

"Ouch! I know. But you're not just any cop."

"Dane doesn't know that."

"No," she agreed. "But I wish I could help him see."

"Maybe we'll find something at the mine that will make it safe for him to come home and clear his name."

She nodded. "I'm ready." She held up a couple of plastic water bottles she had drained earlier. "I'll use these for our samples. We can stop on the way home at an office supply place, print the forms from the phone and pop the samples in the mail."

"Where will you have the results sent?"

"My friend Maisie can receive them. She's sort of helping me. She sent me the correct forms to send off."

"How did she get in touch with you?" he asked.

"I called her on the phone you gave me. But I didn't tell her where I was or mention you at all. And I kept the call short and shut off the phone as soon as I hung up."

He frowned, but all he said was "Let's get going."

They were largely silent on the drive to the mine, weary from the stress of the day, or simply lost in their own thoughts. At one point, Jason reached over and took her hand. He continued to hold it until they turned off the highway, a silent reassurance that lifted some of the fatigue dragging at her.

The road up to the mine was as rough as she remembered, forcing Cara to steady herself with one hand on the dash as the truck rocked through ruts and shuddered across washboarded gravel. Jason swung through the last turn onto the mine road and had to hit the brakes hard to keep from colliding with a large steel gate.

"That wasn't here before," Cara said.

"No. It's new." He indicated the posts supporting the gate. "That concrete looks fresh."

She looked past the gate, to where the road vanished into trees at the top of the hill. "How far from here to the mine?" she asked.

"From what I remember, about a mile." He backed up until he could return the way they had come. "I saw a place I can hide the truck," he said. "About a quarter mile from here. We'll hike in from there."

Wary of being spotted by whomever had shot at them the last time, they left the truck and kept to the thick growth of pinion and cedar to the side of the road. It made for slow going, and Cara was grateful for the lengthening days. Even so, by the time the first waste piles of rock loomed within sight, dusk was descending, washing everything of color and deepening the shadows.

"I'll take one of these," Jason said, hefting a grapefruit-size rock from the top of one pile and stowing it in his pack. Cara knelt at the base of the pile, unscrewed the lid on one of the plastic bottles and trickled in a handful of soil. She wrote "Soil from surface of Mary Lee Mine site" and the date and time of collection on a label she had affixed to the bottle.

"We just need a sample from that creek back there," she said, standing. She turned and was surprised to see that Jason had drawn his weapon. "What is it?" she asked, fear rising in her throat.

"I'm just being cautious." He touched her shoulder. "Stay close. We'll walk together."

Cara strained her ears for the sound of anyone or

anything out of the ordinary, but could only hear her own pounding pulse and the occasional scrape of their footsteps on the rough ground. When they reached the creek, she hurriedly knelt and collected her sample, her hands shaking as she labeled the bottle. She stood and stowed it in the pack. "Let's get out of here," she said.

Then an explosion of tree bark six inches from her right ear stung her face and filled the air with shrieking. Only when Jason grabbed her and tugged her away did she realize she was the one screaming.

JASON RAN, dragging Cara after him. Gunshots pursued them, too close to be intentional misses. Their erratic movements and the growing darkness were probably the only things keeping them alive right now.

But the darkness handicapped them, too. More than once he tripped over tree roots or fallen branches. When Cara went sprawling, he hauled her to her feet and kept running. He'd holstered his weapon, unwilling to stop to try to pinpoint the location of the shooter, knowing it was unlikely he would be able to see whoever it was in the darkness, anyway.

No longer as concerned about concealment now that they had been discovered, when they reached the dirt road that led to the gate, Jason took it, running down one side. The shots that pursued them had stopped, but he knew that didn't mean they had escaped. Sure enough, a few minutes later, the roar of a revving engine tore through the darkness and headlights hit them like a spotlight.

He shoved Cara into the cover of the trees and dove

after her. They ran, then fell, then tumbled down the slope, landing in a heap against the fence. "Are you hurt?" he asked, scrambling to her on his hands and knees.

"No." She shoved herself upright and he did likewise.

"Can you make it over the fence?" he asked. The ground sloped away sharply on this side, making for a longer climb. "The truck isn't far now."

"I can do it if you give me a boost."

He squatted down. "Climb on my back," he said. "I'll lift you up."

She did as he asked. He winced only a little at the feel of her hard boot heel in the small of his back. Then she was up and clambering over the fence. He turned and followed, every nerve on edge, anticipating a bullet striking him in the back.

But no bullet came, though they had to flatten themselves in the shallow roadside ditch as headlights swept over them and a black SUV roared past. They lay in the ditch for many long moments afterward, breathing hard, their only communication through their tightly clasped hands, holding on to each other as if to a lifeline.

Just when he was about to stand, more gunfire exploded—but this time much farther away. "What's happened?" Cara asked, panic edging her words.

"I don't know." Were there pursuers shooting at someone else? Or merely firing at anything that moved?

The shots died away and silence descended. He waited another ten minutes, counting his breaths, then shoved onto his knees. "Come on," he said. "My truck isn't far."

The truck wasn't far, but as the beam of the flashlight he had pulled from his belt played over it, he took in a windshield shattered by bullets, the two front tires shredded by gunfire. Behind him, Cara gasped. "What are we going to do now?"

He took her hand in his and stepped into the road. "The only thing we can do. We walk."

CARA FOLLOWED JASON, though her tired, aching legs protested with every step. Full darkness had descended, making walking away from the road difficult and dangerous. "We'll stay on the side of the road unless we hear a car coming," Jason said. "Then we'll hide in the underbrush. Sound carries out here, so we should have plenty of warning."

"Fine." All the tension of the past few days was catching up to Cara. Dragging her leaden legs along took all her effort.

"When we get a cell signal, I'll call for help," Jason said.

"You can't call the Ranger Brigade," she said. "They'll have to turn me over to the sheriff."

"We'll think of something," he said.

"Who is doing this?" she asked. "What could there possibly be at that old mine site that's worth killing someone?"

Before he could answer her, the low growl of an approaching car drifted up the hill. Jason took her hand once more and they plunged into the underbrush. They crouched in a prickly mass of Gambel oak and stared as the black SUV rumbled past. It moved slowly, the driver scanning the roadside with a hand-held spotlight.

"Down!" Jason ordered, and Cara pressed her face to the dirt beneath the oak brush, eyes tightly closed, so tense with fear, she ached.

The rumble of the engine grew fainter then died altogether. She raised her head and looked toward the darker shadow she knew was Jason. "Whoever that is, he knows we're out here and he's not going to stop looking," she said.

"He's not going to find us," Jason said. "It's a really dark night. A lot of clouds."

She hadn't paid any attention to the weather on the way here. Now she looked up and realized she couldn't see any stars. No wonder they'd had such a hard time finding sure footing. "You say that like all this darkness is a good thing," she said. "We're liable to fall and break an ankle or stumble over a cliff."

"If we stick to the road, we'll be okay," he said. "And searchers aren't likely to venture out on foot in this blackness. If they do, we'll hear them stumbling around in the dark a long time before they find us."

He stood and took her hand, pulling her up alongside him. "I'm scared," she said, leaning against him for a moment. "Those bullets were way too close this time."

"I know," he said. "It scares me, too."

"But you're a cop. You're trained for this kind of thing."

"That doesn't mean I don't get frightened. I've just learned to push past the fear." He kissed her, possibly aiming in the darkness for her cheek, but landing instead on her nose. Still, the contact—and his admission that he was only human—comforted her. They were a team and together they would face whatever was out there.

They set off along the road again. At least they were moving downhill. At least they knew they would reach cell service eventually. Jason wasn't going to turn her over to the sheriff. She had the water and soil samples from the mine, which should tell her if TDC was actually cleaning up the place or only pretending to. She'd find a way to prove her own innocence, and Dane's.

A crack of thunder so loud she felt the rumble beneath her feet made her cry out, followed closely by lightning that lit the sky like a strobe. She turned to Jason, who had his head tilted back, looking up at the sky.

Then the heavens opened and the rain began to pour.

Chapter Nineteen

Jason was beyond wet. Water squelched in his boots and dripped in his hair. It sloshed against his skin, weighing down his clothing and pooling in his ears. Mud dragged at his feet and running water turned the road into a river. Sheets of cold rain made it impossible to see, even when lightning exploded nearby in fiery light.

Cara clutched at his hand and shuffled beside him, bent over, her free arm hugging her body, water sluicing around her like sea spray from a rising mermaid. Each time a flash of lightning illuminated Cara, she looked wetter and more miserable—exactly the way he felt.

"We've got to find shelter," he said, shouting to be heard over the drum of rain.

"Where?" she shouted back.

He thought back to those long-ago Outward Bound expeditions that taught students how to build temporary structures from tree branches and vines. He'd been pretty good at the task back then, but he'd never tried to craft a shelter in the pouring rain, in inky darkness, on the side of a mountain.

"We're already so wet, what difference does it make?" Cara asked.

They could build a fire—provided they could find enough dry wood to do so. He had a tin of matches and a lighter and fire-starters in his pack. But it would take a bonfire to dry out their clothes, and that risked letting their pursuers know exactly where to find them.

He pulled out his phone, switched it on and checked the display. No bars. He switched it off to conserve the battery and slogged forward once more.

"Why is it taking so long to get to the highway?" Cara asked when they had been walking another half hour. "It didn't seem like that far in the car."

"We're traveling a lot slower on foot," he said. "We should be able to see the lights from the highway before long." But another hour passed with no lights and the road got much rougher. They had to navigate around deep ruts running with water and over sections that seemed more jagged rock than road.

"I don't remember any of this," Cara said.

Jason stopped, switched on a flashlight he took from his backpack and shone it around them. The remnants of an old barbwire fence lined one side of the road, while the other side was open fields. Cara touched his arm. "Did we take a wrong turn somewhere?" she asked. "Are we lost?"

"We must have," he said. He'd driven to the mine twice now in daylight, and definitely didn't remember that fence or this road, which was more trail that road. He switched off the light. "We need to find somewhere to stay put until morning," he said. "Then we'll have a better chance of getting our bearings."

"Sure," she said. "I can sit in the pouring rain as well as I can walk in it. You can't really drown in a rainstorm, can you?" Her voice was strained, on the edge of hysteria. Jason didn't blame her. He felt a little out of control himself.

"Let's walk up the road just a little farther, see if we can spot a bunch of trees," he said. "Maybe we can make a shelter." Those skills from his younger years might come in handy, after all.

CARA WAS SURE she was hallucinating when the sheepherder's trailer appeared in a flash of lightning. It hunched at the side of the road, boxy and white, with a curved roof like that on a Gypsy caravan, a silver stovepipe thrusting from the center. She grabbed Jason's arm. "Did you see that?"

"See what?"

She shook her head. "I don't know. I was probably imagining it, but I thought…" Lightning flashed again. "There!" She pointed toward the trailer.

"I see it." He grabbed her hand. "Come on. Let's see if anybody is home."

Up close, the trailer looked deserted—no smoke from the chimney, no lights showing at the windows. Jason knocked and called out, but no one answered. Finally, he took out his pocketknife and pried at the door. "This is an emergency," he said to Cara, and pulled the door open.

The scents of wood smoke and old mothballs greeted

them, but the interior was clean and dry—blessedly dry. A lantern stood on the dinette and Jason lit it, while Cara shook out the blankets from the bed. Two coats hung from pegs on the wall, worn and much-patched, but she didn't care. The blankets and coats were dry and therefore warmer than her own soaked clothing. She was already shivering so violently she could scarcely speak. "Can you…start a fire?" she asked.

He opened the woodstove and peered inside. "Let me see if I can find some dry wood." He shed his pack and went back outside. She checked the cabinets over the small sink and two-burner gas stove and almost wept when she found a can of ground coffee, canned milk and cans of soup. By the time Jason had returned, she had unearthed a can opener and was dumping food into pots. "The stove won't light, so I'm guessing there's no propane," she said. "But we can heat this on the fire once you've got it going."

"I found a bunch of firewood piled around a tree and was able to pull some relatively dry pieces from the middle of the stack," he said, as he dropped the wood on the floor in front of the stove and set to work. "You should get out of those wet clothes," he added, arranging kindling in the stove. "Wrap up in one of those blankets."

He didn't have to tell her twice. By the time he had the fire going, she was curled up at the foot of the bed, a blanket wrapped around her. Her skin was still icy, and her teeth wouldn't stop chattering, but the hope of warmth didn't seem like a faraway dream anymore.

Jason adjusted the stove damper and stood. "That

should start to warm us in a minute." He moved the teakettle she had filled to one side of the stovepipe and set the pot of soup on the other. He arranged her clothes to dry on a kitchen chair off to the side of the stove.

"You need to get out of your wet clothing, too," she said.

"You just want to get me naked and take advantage of me," he said.

"Oh, that's right. I planned all of this—including the weather and the guys with guns—so I could get you to take off your clothes. Because it's so impossible otherwise."

"Well, you know how shy I am." With that, he stripped off his trousers and began wrestling out of his wet shirt. Seconds later, wrapped in the second blanket, he joined Cara on the bed.

"Your skin is like ice," she said, reaching under the blanket to squeeze his thigh.

"So is yours." He moved over, tugged at her blanket and then shifted the coverings so that they were snuggled together, both blankets around them. The contact was almost painful at first, both of them so damp and cold, but the warmth of connection and the heat from the crackling fire in the stove began to seep in, turning pain into pleasure.

"It feels heavenly just to be warm," she said, leaning back against him and admiring the play of flames behind the glass door of the stove.

"Mmm" was his only answer, though his arms around her tightened.

"Are you falling asleep?" she asked.

"No."

She turned toward him and they kissed. Kissing progressed to touching and stroking. They made love leisurely, with no acrobatics or attempts to impress, just a gentle enjoyment of each other's bodies. Men with guns and officers who wanted to arrest her seemed a world away from this peace.

She was almost asleep when he nudged her much later. "The soup and the tea water are boiling," he said.

The words cut through her fatigue and her stomach pinched with hunger. She sat. "I'm starved."

They ate at the little dinette, wrapped in the blankets and inhaling the food—soup, followed by a can of peaches. They took turns slurping the peach juice and grinning at each other. She knew her hair was as messy as his, her face as wind-burned, eyes as bloodshot. But it didn't matter. If she had to be trapped in a sheepherder's trailer with anyone in the world, he was the only one she would choose.

They returned to the bed after they ate. She thought she would sleep but instead she found herself thinking about the day's events, as if now that she was warm, dry and fed, her mind could take in the enormity of what had happened.

"If TDC thought Dane was a terrorist, why not say so at their press conference?" she asked out loud. "Why the sudden flurry of action?"

"Terrorism is a pretty serious charge," Jason said. "Maybe Homeland Security was building their case."

"There is no case. Dane isn't a terrorist. Neither am I."

"All right," Jason said. "What evidence could TDC

have given Homeland Security to persuade them to pursue the case?"

Cara started to argue that TDC didn't have any evidence, but that wasn't what he was asking, was it? She considered the question a moment. "They could have presented federal agents with the reports that showed radioactive material at the Mary Lee Mine, and pointed out that the EPA tests didn't show the same results. Dane was working at that site, so maybe they argued *he* was hiding the radioactive stuff at the mine."

She propped herself up on her elbows. "The problem is, I don't know enough about the science behind all of this to figure out everything those reports say. Dane had a master's degree and years of study in chemistry and biology and other sciences. I can build a database and I know the correct grammar and spelling for reports, and how to arrange a conference call and deal with accounting software, but I can't tell you if just storing yellowcake uranium or whatever it is terrorists use to eventually build a bomb, would result in the kinds of reports we saw."

"I don't think those details matter so much," Jason said. "All I want is to find out who is after us and stop them. Knowing why would be an added bonus, and finding Dane would be the cherry on top of the sundae. But most of all, I want you to be safe."

She laced her fingers with his. "I feel safer with you. But it's hard when I don't know who my enemy is or why they're after me."

"Try to get some sleep. Tomorrow we'll hike back to cell service and get to the bottom of all this."

She knew he meant the words to be reassuring, but returning to town wasn't a comforting idea to her. All that awaited her there were people who wanted to arrest her and put her in jail.

JASON KNEW THEY were in trouble when he woke to the sound of an engine revving and the crunch of tires on gravel. He sat up in bed and reached for his gun before he even put on his clothes. Cara still slept, curled on her side, a lock of hair falling across one cheek.

Their wet clothing had dried, so he quickly dressed and, carrying his boots, slipped to the window and peered out. The black SUV was almost to the trailer, the first rays of the sun glinting off the windshield, making it impossible to see whoever was inside.

"What is it?" Cara spoke from the bed. "Who's out there?"

"You'd better get dressed," he said, keeping his voice low. "We've got company."

"Who is it?"

"It's a black SUV. I can't see who's driving it.".

Cara moved to the now cold woodstove and dressed. "I need to pee," she said.

"You'll have to do it in here," he said. "You can't risk going outside."

She glanced out the small back window over the sink. "They can't see the outhouse from the front of the trailer," she said. "I could slip out there and be back before they knew."

"No. It's too risky."

She didn't argue, though he could tell she wanted to. "What's going on out there?" she asked instead.

"They just parked outside."

She came to stand behind him, her chin resting on his shoulder, her breasts pressed to his back. Two men—Durrell and George—got out of the SUV. "I knew it," she whispered. "So TDC is behind this."

Jason said nothing, merely watched as the two men, dressed in black tactical gear instead of suits, studied the ground around the trailer. He cursed himself for not even making an effort to erase his and Cara's tracks after they'd arrived last night. He had been sure they were too far off any obvious path to be found.

He'd been foolish and careless, and if anything happened to Cara now, it would be his fault.

Durrell looked at George and said something Jason couldn't make out. Then each man drew a handgun and they started toward the trailer, moving at oblique angles. Jason might now have had a chance to take them out, but he couldn't kill two men in cold blood.

"Get under the bed," he told Cara.

She stared at him. "What do you mean? Why?"

"Get under the bed. If they fire on us, you're less likely to be hit there."

"And then I'll be trapped under there. I think if they try to come in this door, we need to go out the back window." She indicated the window over the dinette.

"Does that even open?" he asked.

"I'll find out."

Before he could stop her, she went to the dinette, crawled up on the padded seat and shoved at the window. It flew open, damp, cool air rushing in. "We can fit through it," she said.

He was ready for this to be over. He wanted to stand and face off with these guys. But there were two of them and he only had one gun. "Let's see what they do first," he whispered.

She nodded but remained by the window.

Jason glanced out the front window again and noticed that Durrell was moving around the side of the trailer. He was heading toward the back. They were going to be trapped. "Get out, now!" he said, and rushed toward the rear window.

He shoved Cara out ahead of him and then hit the ground hard beside her. Not stopping to catch his breath, he pulled her up and they began running. Durrell shouted, and fired. Jason searched for cover, but there was none. These open sheep pastures had long been cleared of all but the scrawniest of shrubs.

One moment, Cara was running beside him. The next, she fell. He looked back to see her sprawled on the ground, but before he could retrace his steps, Durrell was on her. He grabbed her up and hauled her roughly to her feet.

George, who had quickly caught up with Durrell, stopped and aimed his weapon at Jason. "Stop, or you're a dead man," he shouted.

"Jason, stop!" Cara called.

He didn't stop. Not because he wanted to leave Cara alone with those two, but because he had seen something she hadn't. Durrell had gripped Cara to him and fumbled in his back pocket to take out a rope. Not flexicuffs or even old-fashioned handcuffs, but a rope. That wasn't the tool a law enforcement officer would use, not even one under cover. A chill had swept over him at the sight and, with it, the certainty that these men weren't making an arrest or intending to take Cara into to custody.

They were killers, and if Jason let them get hold of him, he would have no way of saving Cara.

INSTEAD OF PURSUING Jason, Durrell turned back to Cara. "We'll take care of him later," he said. "He isn't going to go far out here."

Durrell pulled her wrists together behind her and wrapped them with the rope, the coarse fiber digging into her skin. "Let's go," he said, and tugged her back toward the trailer.

Inside the trailer, Durrell threw Cara onto the bed. She landed on her side, and lay staring up at them, her wrists bound behind her. "Who are you?" she asked. "What do you want with me?"

Both men ignored the question. Durrell looked around the small trailer, then dragged one of the two chairs into the center of the room. George went outside and returned a few moments later with a longer coil of rope. He studied the ceiling, then shook his head. "We'll have to do it over the door," he said.

"That's even better," Durrell said. "No fancy knots." He dragged the chair over in front of the door.

George moved over to the bed and pulled Cara to her feet. "Come over here," he said, and dragged her toward the chair.

"What are you doing?" she asked, fear rising to almost choke her.

"Climb up on the chair," Durrell ordered.

She stared at him. He hit her, hard. Her head snapped back and her vision blurred.

"What did you do that for?" George asked.

"When I give an order, I expect to be obeyed," he said.

"You shouldn't leave marks. The local cops might be smarter than we think."

"Get on the chair," Durrell said again.

Cara sat on the chair. Her face hurt where he had hit her, but the pain helped her push back some of her fear. She had worked so hard after Corey died to build a new life, with a new job, a new home. A life that didn't require her to care too much or risk getting hurt. Jason, and even Dane, had changed that. They had made her care, and now these two, and whoever they worked for, were trying to shut her down. Rage welled at the thought. She wasn't going to let that happen. She couldn't let them win.

"Don't sit!" Durrell ordered. "Stand on it."

Moving awkwardly with her bound hands, she climbed onto the chair. Behind her, George did something with the long rope, then he looped one end around her neck and fumbled behind her. "What are you doing?" she asked.

"You're distraught that the Feds have found out about your collusion with Dane Trask to sell nuclear material to foreign terrorists," Durrell said. "So you came to this deserted place and hanged yourself."

"No! I didn't collude with Dane. He didn't do anything wrong. And I would never kill myself."

"Then we'll do the job for you, but the authorities won't know any different," Durrell said. He looked at his partner. "Is everything ready?"

"I think so," George said.

"Wait," she cried. "At least tell me why you're doing this."

"Short answer—because you got nosy," Durrell said. "You got curious about things you never should have worried about. Now we need you out of the way." He looked to George. "You want to pull the chair out from under her or should I do it?"

"You do it. She's probably going to kick and I want to be out of the way."

"Wuss," Durrell said, but took a step toward Cara.

She decided when he jerked the chair away, she would kick him as hard as she could, aiming for the teeth. It might not save her, but at least he'd walk around for a while with some evidence of what he had done.

Where are you, Jason? she thought. *I hope you're far away by now, and safe. And I hope you know how much I love you, even if I never got a chance to say it.*

JASON SLOWED, fighting for breath, pain stabbing his side. He strained his ears, listening for sounds of pursuit. After the first few shots, George hadn't bothered wasting his ammunition. But why hadn't he come after Jason?

Because he was in a hurry to get back to the trailer,

and Cara. The thought sent a chill through him and he began retracing his steps toward the trailer.

He approached the site at an angle, keeping to the cover of rocks and out of view of the trailer's windows. When he was very close, he used Durrell and George's SUV as a shield. Scuffling noises came from inside the trailer. Thoughts of what they might be doing to Cara made his hands shake with rage, and he forced himself to push the emotion aside. He had to put on his cop face now, focus on the job, save emotion for later. He reviewed the layout of the trailer in his mind. No back door. The window he and Cara had exited through was too far off the ground to make climbing back in practical. He'd have to enter by the front door, and hope he could catch Durrell and George by surprise, taking them out before they had a chance to hurt Cara.

A lot of ifs. What he needed was some kind of distraction—something that would make Durrell and George leave the trailer in a hurry. He moved along the side of the SUV until he reached the driver's door and tried the handle. To his surprise, the door was unlocked. He eased it open and peered inside. No keys in the ignition, so there went the idea of starting up the vehicle to get them to run out to see who was stealing their ride.

Two water bottles rested in the center console. A phone charger. A spare ammunition clip on the passenger's-side floorboard. A lighter and a package of cigarettes on the dashboard.

He grabbed the lighter, the smokes, and the ammo clip and hurried behind the trailer, to a spot in a depression about a hundred yards away. Hastily, he scraped together dried grass and twigs and touched them with the lighter flame. They flared, and he fed in larger twigs, until he had a small but healthy blaze going. Then he emptied the contents of the ammunition clip into the fire and raced back around to the front of the trailer.

Ammunition in a campfire didn't usually shoot out like fireworks, but when those bullets gassed off and exploded, they would sound like a barrage of gunfire directly behind the trailer. As Jason had hoped, when the explosions sounded, it only took about fifteen seconds for Durrell and George to exit the trailer and run for their SUV. They dove into the vehicle and George started it.

Jason's first shot punctured the left front tire. "Don't move!" he ordered, rising up alongside the driver's side. He held his Glock in both hands, aimed directly at George's face. No way could he miss from here. When Durrell raised his gun, Jason fired, shattering the front windshield and sending shards raining over both men. Still keeping the gun trained on them, he yanked open the driver's door and dragged George out of the vehicle. "Down on the ground, now!" he shouted. "Both of you."

George lay with his face in the dirt, but Durrell made a run for the trailer. Jason fired, catching him in the shoulder. He went down, screaming.

Within minutes, Jason had them both bound hand and foot, had frisked them and removed their weapons before racing for the trailer.

Cara was standing on a chair, a loop of rope around her neck, her expression resolute. He had to climb onto the chair with her to free her. She sagged against him. "What took you so long?" she choked out as he worked on loosening the rope from around her neck.

"I had to deal with a couple of guys," he said, and pulled the rope from around her neck, then went to work cutting loose her hands.

When she was free, she wrapped her arms around him and they held each other tightly, standing on a chair in that isolated sheepherder's trailer.

Durrell began bellowing. "Come on." Jason jumped to the floor and reached up to help Cara down. "We've got to deal with those two."

She shrank back. "What are you going to do?"

"Durrell is injured. He was headed for the trailer and you, so I shot him. I'd better get out there and tend to him before he bleeds out."

She didn't question the irony that he had shot a man to stop him—and would have killed him if necessary—but would now do all he could to save his life. She merely went to the corner shelves, retrieved a stack of towels and followed him outside.

Durrell had almost stopped bleeding by the time they got to him, but he shouted curses and thrashed around until Jason took out his handkerchief and gagged him. He fished a wallet from the guy's pocket and found IDs for Anthony Durrell, Tony Green and David Turner. "Which one is your real name?" he asked. But Durrell only glared at him.

George lay quietly on his side. Jason examined his wallet, which had identification for Walter George and George Walters. But he, too, refused to answer when

Jason questioned him. So Jason and Cara dragged first George, and then Durrell, over to the black SUV and loaded them inside, Durrell in the rear of the vehicle and George strapped into the back seat. It was like maneuvering two big sacks of cement, and both he and Cara were sweating by the time they were done.

"I'll be so glad to get out of here," Cara said.

"Me, too." Jason handed her the Glock.

She took it gingerly. "What do you want me to do with this?"

"Keep an eye on those two." He nodded toward the rear of the SUV. "If they try anything, just pull the trigger." He didn't think that would be necessary, but he wanted Durrell and George to hear the words and believe he meant them.

Cara nodded. "What are you going to do?"

"I have to change a tire." Then he was going to drive them all to safety and, he hoped, a lot of long-overdue answers.

THEY DIDN'T GET to Montrose until midafternoon. Jason pulled in behind the sheriff's office building and called in to let them know he was outside with two criminals. By the time four deputies emerged, he and Cara were standing outside the vehicle. One of the deputies approached Cara, restraints in hand.

She forced herself to remain still, not cowering behind Jason. "Not her," Jason said before she could speak. "The two men in the car. They tried to kill us twice, and were preparing to fake Ms. Mead's suicide."

She rubbed at the faint rope burn around her neck and continued to glare at the deputy.

"Ms. Mead is the one we have a warrant for," the deputy said.

"She's in my custody at the moment, so if you want a chance at her, you'll have to wait in line," Jason said.

Cara bit her lip to keep from crying out. Could Jason, a federal officer, really claim priority over the local cops? This whole situation was absurd, so why not?

"Who are these two?" asked a second deputy who was standing beside the black SUV, surveying its remaining occupants.

Jason took out the two wallets and handed them to the first officer. "They both have multiple IDs. My guess is their real names are something else entirely. But most recently, they've been masquerading as Anthony Durrell and Walter George, employees of TDC Enterprises."

"But they aren't really TDC employees?" the first man asked.

"You'll have to take that up with TDC," Jason said.

Cara was still nervous about walking into the sheriff's department, but she had no intention of leaving Jason's side, so she went with him when they followed the cops inside.

It took several hours to tell their story, starting with Dane Trask's disappearance, through the harassment and vandalism of Cara's home, the shots fired on them during their first visit to the Mary Lee Mine, and the mad chase through the darkness on their second visit.

Cara couldn't tell how much the detectives interviewing them believed, but they recorded every word, asked a lot of questions, and didn't try to take her into custody when it came time for them to leave.

"We may have more questions for you later," her chief questioner said. "But for now, we're releasing you into Officer Beck's custody."

"I promise to keep a close eye on her," Jason said solemnly.

She waited until they were in the pickup before she punched him—lightly—on the shoulder.

"Hey! What was that for?" He rubbed his shoulder.

"That crack about keeping a close eye on me. Honestly!"

"I was only stating the truth." He grinned. "Ready to go back to my place?"

"Let's get these samples in the mail," she said, holding up the backpack she'd retrieved before they'd left the trailer. "I still want to know what they show."

They stopped by an office supply store to print the forms, mailed the samples, then headed for Jason's cabin.

WHILE CARA HAD showered, Jason had grilled steaks and opened a bottle of Pinot Noir.

Cara gratefully took a glass. "Let's not talk about the case tonight," he said.

She clinked her glass to his. "Deal." She sipped the wine and sighed. "So what should we talk about?"

"How about the future?"

She made a face. "I'll have to find a new job. I want to go back to my house, but I'm not sure how long it will be before I feel safe there again. And Dane is still missing, and I'm worried about him."

Jason pulled her into his arms and kissed her. "You'll find a new job because you're good at what you do," he said. "You don't have to go back to your house until you're ready. You can stay here as long as you like. And we're going to keep looking for Dane. So far, he's been doing a good job of staying safe and looking after himself. Remember that."

She studied him, eyes searching. "You're the man with all the answers, aren't you?"

"Right now, I have a question?"

"Oh?" A tremor went through her—excitement. Anticipation. Fear?

"I love you. You know that, don't you?"

She nodded. Then added, "Yes. I love you, too." She gave a nervous laugh. "That was the last thing I expected, I tell you."

"What would you think about us getting married?"

Cara's heart stopped beating for a moment. She stared at him. "Married?"

"When you're ready. Sooner rather than later, I hope." He took her wineglass and his and set them aside, and held both her hands in his. "I want to spend the rest of my life with you."

"Yes," she whispered. Then, with more force, "Yes!" Happiness swelled in her like a balloon, as if she might float into the air without his hands to tether her.

Two DAYS LATER, lab results showed traces of tritium and uranium in the soil samples recovered from the Mary Lee Mine—very different from the test results TDC had released to the public earlier.

The real identities of Anthony Durrell and Walter George turned out to be David Alexander and Kerry Waters, respectively—hired killers. TDC Enterprises issued an official statement that they had no knowledge of any of this, that the two men had presented themselves as private security.

TDC also denied any knowledge of how radioactive materials got into the Superfund Mary Lee Mine's soil and water samples. The company continued to attest that Dane Trask put the material there, though they had no explanation as to how the material would have gotten there in the quantities found. They would certainly launch an immediate investigation.

Homeland Security and the Montrose County Sheriff's Office withdrew any charges against Cara. Rather than wait to be fired from TDC, she quit and took a job with an environmental group that was threatening a lawsuit against TDC. Though the position paid less than her old job, once she sold her house and moved in permanently with Jason, her finances would be in better shape than ever.

Dane was still missing, but Durrell and George—or rather, Alexander and Waters—were behind bars, and TDC was pledging to clean up the Mary Lee Mine site. And, as Jason had said, Dane had the skills to look after himself and would no doubt come forward when he felt safe again.

Meanwhile, Cara had a wedding to plan, and a future that included putting a lot more trust in law enforcement than she had ever thought possible.

* * * * *

*Look for the next book in Cindi Myers's
The Ranger Brigade: Rocky Mountain Manhunt
when* Mountain of Evidence *is available
in December 2020,
only from Harlequin Intrigue!*

WE HOPE YOU ENJOYED
THIS BOOK FROM
⬡ HARLEQUIN
INTRIGUE

Seek thrills. Solve crimes. Justice served.

Dive into action-packed stories that will keep you
on the edge of your seat. Solve the crime
and deliver justice at all costs.

6 NEW BOOKS AVAILABLE EVERY MONTH!

SPECIAL EXCERPT FROM

(H) HARLEQUIN

INTRIGUE

*Sheriff Colton O'Connor is stunned when a stormy night
brings him face-to-face with a woman from his past.
Seeing Makena Eden again is a shock to his system...
especially once he realizes she's hiding something. As
the rain turns torrential, Colton has to get to the heart
of what Makena is doing in his small hometown. And
why her once-vibrant eyes look so incredibly haunted...*

Keep reading for a sneak peek at
Texas Law, *part of An O'Connor Family Mystery,*
from USA TODAY *bestselling author Barb Han.*

Makena needed medical attention. That part was obvious. The
tricky part was going to be getting her looked at. He was still
trying to wrap his mind around the fact Makena Eden was
sitting in his SUV.

Talk about a blast from the past and a missed opportunity.
But he couldn't think about that right now when she was injured.
At least she was eating. That had to be a good sign.

When she'd tried to stand, she'd gone down pretty fast and
hard. She'd winced in pain and he'd scooped her up and brought
her to his vehicle. He knew better than to move an injured
person. In this case, however, there was no choice.

The victim was alert and cognizant of what was going on.
A quick visual scan of her body revealed nothing obviously
broken. No bones were sticking out. She complained about her
hip and he figured there could be something there. At the very
least, she needed an X-ray.

Since getting to the county hospital looked impossible at least in the short run and his apartment was close by, he decided taking her to his place might be for the best until the roads cleared. He could get her out of his uncomfortable vehicle and onto a soft couch.

Normally, he wouldn't take a stranger to his home, but this was Makena. And even though he hadn't seen her in forever, she'd been special to him at one time.

He still needed to check on the RV for Mrs. Dillon…and then it dawned on him. Was Makena the "tenant" the widow had been talking about earlier?

"Are you staying in town?" he asked, hoping to get her to volunteer the information. It was possible that she'd fallen on hard times and needed a place to hang her head for a couple of nights.

"I've been staying in a friend's RV," she said. So, she was the "tenant" Mrs. Dillon had mentioned.

It was good seeing Makena again. At five feet five inches, she had a body made for sinning underneath a thick head of black hair. He remembered how shiny and wavy her hair used to be. Even soaked with water, it didn't look much different now.

She had the most honest set of pale blue eyes—eyes the color of the sky on an early summer morning. She had the kind of eyes that he could stare into all day. It had been like that before, too.

But that was a long time ago. And despite the lightning bolt that had struck him square in the chest when she turned to face him, this relationship was purely professional.

Don't miss
Texas Law *by Barb Han,*
available December 2020 wherever
Harlequin Intrigue books and ebooks are sold.

Harlequin.com

IF YOU ENJOYED THIS BOOK
WE THINK YOU WILL ALSO LOVE

LOVE INSPIRED SUSPENSE
INSPIRATIONAL ROMANCE

Courage. Danger. Faith.

Find strength and determination in stories
of faith and love in the face of danger.

6 NEW BOOKS AVAILABLE EVERY MONTH!

SPECIAL EXCERPT FROM

LOVE INSPIRED SUSPENSE
INSPIRATIONAL ROMANCE

*A deputy must protect a baby and
her new temporary guardian.*

Read on for a sneak preview of
Christmas Protection Detail *by Terri Reed,*
available December 2020 from Love Inspired Suspense.

"I'm going to find her." Nick Delaney shrugged off her hand. "She needs help."

"You're a civilian. Somebody trained to provide help needs to go," Deputy Kaitlin Lanz replied.

He flashed her one of his smiles, but it didn't dispel the anxiety in his eyes. "Then we can go together."

Digging his keys from his coat pocket, he held them out to her. "You can drive my Humvee. It's better equipped than yours."

"Fine." She plucked the keys from his hand.

"Come with me," Kaitlin said to Nick. Instead of immediately going out the door, Kaitlin stopped where the department's tactical gear was stored. She grabbed a duty belt and two flak vests. She tossed one to Nick. "Put that on."

Velcroing her vest in place, she grabbed her department-issue shearling jacket and put it on, covering her sweater. "Let's roll."

Once they were settled in the large SUV, Kaitlin fired up the engine and drove through town. Within moments, she turned onto the long winding road that led up the second-tallest mountain in the county. The bright headlights of the SUV cut through the darkness and bounced off the snow. They'd reached the summit near the gate of the estate when the SUV's headlights swung across the accident scene. A dark gray sedan with chains on the tires had slid off the road into a tree.

Nearby, a black SUV was parked at an angle and two men were dragging a female from the sedan's driver's seat. Kaitlin's hands gripped the steering wheel as she brought the vehicle to an abrupt halt.

Nick popped open his door and slid out.

"Wait!" Kaitlin yelled at him. The fine hairs at her nape quivered.

Were these men Good Samaritans? Or something far more sinister?

The men let go of the woman, letting her flop into the snow. Then both men swiveled to aim high-powered handguns at them.

"Take cover!" Kaitlin reached for the duty weapon at her side. She'd wanted Nick to appreciate her for the capable deputy she was, but not at the risk of his life.

Don't miss
Christmas Protection Detail *by Terri Reed,*
available wherever Love Inspired Suspense books
and ebooks are sold.

LoveInspired.com